PLUSH ZERO

PLUSH ZERO

TYLER H. JOLLEY

H. L. ANDERSON

JOLLEY CHRONICLES

THIS GOES TO ALL THE STUFFED ANIMALS THAT SLEPT IN MY
BED WITH ME WHILE I WAS GROWING UP.

HERE'S TO YOU SHARKEY, WINDOW, AND TREE.

CHAPTER

The "c" in the lighted "Stop a Sec" sign flickered in the waning light of dusk as Covie White pulled up to the pumps at the automated gas station and convenience store. She put the car in park and shut off the engine.

"Mommy! Mommy! Can we go try the claw machine?" Emily begged.

Covie smiled at her daughter, glad she still found joy in toys and games at the age of ten. So many children her age tried to grow up too fast. "Sure. Just let me get this started."

Leaving the nozzle in the gas tank, she let the pump to do its thing as they went inside the seedy gas station. Emily hurried to the claw machine, stamped with the bright purple "Certified Safe Stuffing" sticker, while Covie looked around at the mostly empty shelves in the self-service, scan-and-go store.

"Mommy, it has Daddy's sticker on it! I want one, and there's a walrus in there!" Emily bounced on her toes in front of the game. "The kids said that it's rare!"

Stepping up beside her daughter, Covie eyed the pile

of stuffed animals warily behind the scratched plexiglass. The neon light buzzed and flickered overhead. Safe Stuffing plush were a thing of the past. A large neon-pink notice stuck to the plexiglass between a half-scratched-off narwhal sticker and a unicorn sticker said, "The plush toys in this claw machine were created by Tippy Toys using Safe Stuffing and are guaranteed safe from animation. These stuffed animals will NOT come to life. Guaranteed!"

Covie shook her head and frowned. Before this odd pandemic, where stuffed animals all over the world became animated, that notice would have been considered utter nonsense—something out of a cartoon or horror novel. More likely the latter.

But living, breathing plushies were real, and they were delinquents. And most were dangerous thugs.

Emily pulled on Covie's shirt and pointed. "See him, Mommy? That's the one I want. The walrus."

The machine hummed to life when Covie swiped her debit card. Tippy Toys, with her husband as project manager, thought that creating plush safe for kids to play with was a good way to flip off all the animated plush around the world. But even with Tippy Toys' hubris, not everyone jumped to the idea of having a plush in their vicinity and the project soon crashed and burned, leaving abandoned claw machines all over the world.

But now to Covie's surprise, Safe Stuffing plush were "rare" and "collectible," according to Emily.

Covie, Tom, and Emily weren't afraid of the Safe Stuffing plush, so every now and again, Covie would try her luck on a discarded claw machine just to keep Emily smiling. She maneuvered the claw over the desired toy, but when it dropped, it closed over the black-and-white panda next to the walrus. As the crane-like claw moved the bear toward the prize drawer, Emily crossed her arms and frowned.

"I'm sorry, Em, but it's better than nothing. We're lucky to even have stuffed animals in the world anymore and should be thankful to your dad's company that we do." Covie opened the flap and grabbed the panda from the prize bin. A flash of burning pain shot through the palm of her hand and she dropped the panda on the filthy floor. The stuffed animal melted into a putrid pile of rot that dried quickly into a mass of colorful rainbow charcoal.

Emily backed away, gazing wide-eyed at the odd phenomenon taking place in front of her. The little girl stared from her mom's palm to her eyes.

"What in the world was that?!" Covie whispered, looking at her scorched palm.

Emily sidled up, stopping right behind her, and Covie laid her hand on the girl's shoulder to shield her from the pile of ash that moments before had been a plush bear.

As they stood in shocked silence, an old boxy TV mounted to the ceiling began to broadcast a news program. Covie adjusted her position so she could look at the cracked screen, still see the panda-turned-ash out of the corner of her eye, and continue to protect her daughter from anything that might mutate from it now.

"The most recent plush attack occurred in the middle of Dia Metro City this afternoon when a gang of small yellow penguin plushies broke into a sporting goods store." The reporter paused as footage from the store's security cameras played. "As you can see, the plush are becoming more emboldened, frequently committing crimes in broad daylight."

Covie shook her head. "Let's go finish gassing up and

head home." She held Emily's hand as they walked to the car.

"I really wanted that walrus." Emily pouted. "And then I didn't even get the panda."

Covie stared at her painful red palm for a few seconds.

"Can I ride in the front seat?" Emily asked as they approached the car.

"Sure." Covie smiled.

Emily pulled her hand out of her mom's, jogged the rest of the way to the car, climbed in, and shut the door as Covie removed the nozzle from her tank. Turning to put it back in its place at the pump, she gripped it tighter and backed up against the passenger door. They were surrounded. A gang of plush animals the size of small children crept forward from nearby bushes.

Covie's eyes darted from a tattered stuffed bear holding a wooden board with bent nails sticking out the end to a kitten with a single big eye who had one of only three paws cocked back, with claws made out of toothpicks extended, ready to throw the rock it held. A flopping narwhal, red stuffing dripping from its missing eye, thrashed its head around menacingly, a rusty steak knife duct-taped to its horn. A trio of tigers dripping blood-colored stuffing from various wounds crouched as if ready to pounce, each holding some sort of crude weapon: a short length of rope, a broken bottle, and a tangle of barbed wire wrapped around the third one's frayed tail.

The twenty or so plush encircled Covie, Emily, and the car, growling out threats as they closed in.

CHAPTER TWO

A filthy unicorn, which once had fluffy fur but was now matted with a wet sticky stubstance, parted the group.

"You and you—go to the flank," the unicorn ordered the narwhal and group of tigers with a voice that sounded muffled, like a mouth full of wet cotton.

"Emily, stay in the car!" Covie backed up.

Without any warning, the mangy unicorn charged her with a Chinese throwing star tied to its horn with purple twine. At the last second, Covie kicked, sending the star flying into the tigers a few feet away. Red stuffing stuck to the toe of her favorite workout shoe, and she narrowed her eyes at the oncoming plush.

Covie's toned arms and legs shot out at the nightmarish stuffed animals as she channeled her kickboxing instructor. The trio of tigers recovered from their collision with the unicorn and attacked in a rush of fake fur and missing body parts. She aimed the gas pump nozzle and sprayed them with unleaded, the pungent liquid splashing not only the targeted plush, but her sneakers and the legs of her tight yoga pants as well.

Emily's muffled screams reached Covie through the bulletproof windows of the car—she was suddenly thankful her husband had insisted on them. She dropped the nozzle and, throttling the neck of a stuffed giraffe that jumped at her, sprinted to the other side of the car. She threw the giraffe into the bushes and yanked at the driver's side door, cursing as she ripped a nail off on her already injured hand, and cursing louder when the door failed to open.

Locked. She felt her pockets, then looked through the window into the car. The keyless fob that started the car and unlocked the doors peeked at her from the cup holder next to her screaming daughter.

The plush honed in on Emily, leaping at her window and climbing all over the car. The bear stood on the hood, slamming his nail-embedded board into the windshield over and over. Behind him came what looked like his entourage—a group of at least eight small blue bears mimicking his moves. As more plush piled on, they rocked the car back and forth.

Turning frightened, tearful eyes toward Covie, Emily screamed, "Mommy!"

With the entire gang focused on breaching the car, Covie ran back into the gas station and grabbed the first thing she could use as a weapon: an empty rack that used to display sunglasses. Her heart pounded against her ribs, anger fueling her movements. She rushed back outside, barely registering a computerized voice saying, "Item not identified, please find a scannable item to purchase."

The unorganized crew of plush continued their attack on the car, inadvertently working against each other as they pushed from both sides, trying to topple the vehicle. The lurching narwhal swung its steak-knifed horn into the kitten, knocking one of its eyes asunder with a crack and a spray of putrid fluid.

Covie descended on several plush trying to pry the driver's side door open with a plastic window squeegee. She swung the sunglasses rack like a baseball bat and swiped three of them into the street, then a stuffed weasel with more threadbare bald spots than fake fur became tangled in the wire rack and hissed profanities at her as she pummeled him and two other plush to a pulp on the asphalt. Her side of the car free from attackers, Covie pounded on the window and shouted, "Emily! Unlock my door!" as she pointed to the manual button by the window.

Emily lunged over the center console and unlocked the door. As soon as it clicked, Covie flung it open and climbed in, slamming it shut and hitting the lock before she'd even settled into the seat. "Seat belt!" she yelled to her daughter as she started the engine. The tires squealed as Covie tore out of there, running over plush that got in her way.

The bear plush, still on the hood, lost hold of its weapon and fell, grabbing onto the windshield wiper in front of Emily as its little blue friends flew off the car in all directions. Covie flipped on the wipers with an angry growl, and the bear was flung through the air as the blade it clung to made a rapid arc. It left behind an arm, anchored beneath the rubber strip of the wiper. Emily gagged as cotton stuffing dripping with red blood smeared across her side of the windshield with every swipe of the wiper blade.

Covie glanced in the rearview mirror as she turned onto the road. Clumps of gore-soaked cotton stuffing stretched across the asphalt around the gas pumps. A streak of cottony guts in the shape of a tire track ended at a writhing, flattened gray plush shark. She smiled grimly as it snapped its jaws open and closed against harmless teeth made of felt.

Covie tucked a blanket around Emily where she lounged on the couch. "Watch your show while Dad and I go out to take a look at the car." She kissed her daughter on the forehead, then gestured with a jerk of her head for her husband to follow her.

"What's going on?" he asked. "What happened?"

"I'll explain in the garage." Covie glanced pointedly toward Emily before stepping into the kitchen.

Tom followed obediently as she opened the door into the garage, flipped the light on, stomped down the three steps, and went to stand next to her car. She gestured at the bloody teddy-bear arm still trapped beneath the windshield wiper blade.

"Oh." Tom took a step back, brushing nonexistent detritus from the front of his perfectly white lab coat. "Uhh, I'm sorry?"

Covie told him about the plush gang ambush. "I'm just glad Em was inside the car before they reached us. And thank goodness you insisted on having bulletproof windows installed."

"I'm just glad I'm married to a savage." Tom leaned in to kiss her, but she turned away.

"Ouch," he said.

"That's not the biggest issue." Covie showed him the tender red skin on the palm of her hand. "I want to ask you about this."

Taking her hand, he gently examined it under the dim garage light. "It looks like a burn. How did it happen?"

"One of those Safe Stuffing plush just, I don't know, shocked me? Then it sort of melted into smelly mush and turned to ash when I dropped it."

He frowned. "Well, that doesn't make any sense."

Covie pulled her hand away from him and let her irritation show in the harsh tone of her voice. "I know!" She stomped over to the car and pulled the plush arm from the wiper.

"I forget those things are so bloody." Tom squinted. "Here, let me do that."

Before he could take the appendage from her, Covie threw it on the floor of the garage with a splat. "Yeah, *that* doesn't make any sense either."

"We studied the blood stuffing," Tom said. "That was the first thing I did in the Biotoy division, remember? The results were inconclusive. I mean, there's some structured nucleic-acid pairs, but nothing we've seen on this Earth. It's truly a new disease. And no one has been able to trace what it is. Who knows why there's so much blood? It's some sort of biological component that I'm going to find the cure to!"

Covie smiled. "Okay, I love when you talk all sciencey. But what am I going to do about my hand?"

"I suppose we can treat it like a burn," Tom said, turning back to the house. "You said the machine shocked you?"

"No, the Safe Stuffing plush."

"The actual stuffed animal shocked you?"

"Yes!"

Tom shook his head. "Crazy. Okay. Why do you mess with those things anyway?"

Covie shrugged. "Emily likes to get them when we go out, I don't know. It's like a mommy-daughter thing, I guess, and she said the kids at school said that the walrus is rare and there it was. Sitting in one of those stupid abandoned machines."

"I see," Tom said. "When Safe Stuffing went under, I told the company to take all the claw machines away."

"Well, they didn't. And therein lies the mommy-daughter date thing. I always trusted the Safe Stuffing, Tom, even when it first came out, but now I'll stay away from it. And tell Tippy Toys to get rid of those machines. If it happened to me, then it'll happen to someone else."

"I'll send a memo out first thing in the morning."

Covie walked into the house and Tom slapped her on her butt. She turned around and gave him a hug, and they kissed in the mudroom before going into the kitchen.

CHAPTER THREE

"Cove." Tom reached for her hand again. "I'm sorry. I'll figure this out."

Covie took a deep breath and relaxed her shoulders. She looked up at the handsome man she'd married over twelve years ago. She'd just been happy to find a date who was taller than her back then—not an easy task for a five-foot-ten woman—but she'd quickly fallen in love with more than his height and perfectly parted, shiny hair.

She tugged on the collar of the lab coat that seemed to just be a part of him nowadays, ever since he'd vowed to wear one of many identical jackets until a cure for the plush pandemic was found. "I know you will. I can see the genius wheels turning behind your eyes already." She furrowed her brow and stared at her reddened hand as he held it. "Do you think there was something wrong with the claw machine?"

"I don't know. Maybe." He shook his head. "I still can't believe they weren't decommissioned."

"They're still everywhere." Covie winced as Tom applied ointment from the medicine cabinet. "That's what made it so fun. Em and I would go out to get gas, food, or whatever. We would find a claw machine. It was like a treasure hunt for her. It's Safe Stuffing, for hell's sake! How could this happen?"

He let go of her hand and wiped the excess ointment on a paper towel. "There. That should help."

Covie rested her head back on the couch as her fingers deftly undid the braids in Emily's hair. "All done. Now go brush your teeth and get your PJs on. I'll be there in a minute to read you a story."

"Okay, Mommy."

Tom had disappeared into his den right after they'd eaten dinner. Covie had thought he'd been obsessed with his work as a toy designer/scientist when he'd been assigned to the Safe Stuffing branch of the company. For years, he toiled under the hubris of the board of directors. "We aren't going to live in a world without stuffed animals," they'd say. They were convinced that even though the threat of being attacked by an infected plush existed in the world, people would buy Safe Stuffing stuffed animals.

And the board was right. It made the company thrive for a time and made Tom and Covie comfortable. Tippy Toys adopted the idea that Safe Stuffing was the middle finger to the plush pandemic. But ever since the company moved him over to the Biotoy department to work on finding a cure, it had taken over his life. Their lives.

Covie sighed and pushed herself up off the couch, wincing as her burned palm touched the upholstery. Thankfully, Emily chose a short book for her bedtime story. Covie wasn't at her best as she read to her daughter, distracted by the throbbing in her hand. She kept glancing at her reddened palm, her mind wandering from the words on the page.

"Mom"—Emily took the book out of her hands—"you're reading it wrong. Let me read it to you."

She smiled at her daughter. "That's a wonderful idea, sweetheart. Thank you."

A short while later, story time was over, and Covie tucked Emily in with a kiss to her cheek and shut the door before heading to the bathroom. Her thoughts spun as she brushed her teeth, reliving the plush attack in her mind, wondering what the shock from the supposedly safe panda meant. She scrubbed the makeup off her face and decided she was not going to be able to sleep with everything roiling around in her head.

She needed to talk to Tom. She knocked on the door to his den before entering. "Hey, babe. Can we talk for a minute?"

"Hmm? Yeah, sure." He didn't turn away from his computer as he answered.

Looking at her hand for what had to be the thousandth time since the claw machine incident, she said, "Now that you've had a little time to process it, what do you think happened with the claw machine plush today?"

Still looking at his monitor, he clicked a couple of keys, then wrote something down on a notepad sitting to the right of him. Finally tearing his eyes away from his work, he glanced at Covie over his shoulder before turning back to the computer. He smiled. "I don't know, but I'll look into it. I promise. I'm sure it's nothing."

"Do you . . . I mean, you don't think it had something to do with the Safe Stuffing, do you? Like a rotten batch or something? That claw machine has probably been there for over two years."

"Cove." He turned to face her, finally abandoning his work for a minute. "Do you know how hard I worked on getting that formula just right back then before it was canceled?" He twisted back to face the computer screen. "I'm confident it had nothing to do with the Safe Stuffing, no matter how old it is."

She'd struck a nerve. "I know, Tom. I'm just trying to make sense of it."

He sighed and stared at the J key on his keyboard. "I'm sorry I snapped at you. I'm wondering if your reaction to the plushie has something to do with the injections you've been getting for your Plathos Disease."

She wrinkled her brow with a frown. "Why would that be the cause? What's the connection? Plus, I've held Safe Stuffing plush before and nothing has happened like this."

He shrugged. "It's just a thought. All of these things—the infected plush, the Safe Stuffing plush, and Plathos—are related, in that they all have something to do with DNA, so maybe the synthetic DNA in your shots reacted to something in the Safe Stuffing. Though, I haven't heard any reports of the stuffing being a problem."

He tapped a finger on his desk. "Phyzcoxin is a fairly new medication, and because of the urgency involved with finding an effective treatment, there wasn't time for them to do a lot of testing before rolling it out."

Covie was glad the FDA hadn't dragged their feet with that one. If they had, she might no longer exist, literally. She shuddered as she remembered the doctor's explanation of how Plathos Disease unraveled a person's DNA. Her focus was no longer on her sore hand, but rather on the thought of her DNA unraveling. She just hoped if it ever happened, no one would be around to witness it.

CHAPTER FOUR

Covie sat with her husband in silence for much longer than she felt comfortable before she veered to a different, but related, subject. "Those infected plush came out of nowhere today, like they were just waiting to ambush us. They are getting bolder by the day. Especially here in the city."

"Yes, well, you'll have that with beings that think they can't die."

In the early days of the plush pandemic, the military had been called on to rid the world of the animated plush. Covie remembered watching the videos on the news of the Army blasting a large group of plush that had ransacked the toy store where they'd recently been nothing but regular, inanimate stuffed animals. But before the smoke had cleared, the plush—now missing limbs and chunks of fur, blood-red stuffing oozing out of rips in their bodies—started moving. Some moved quickly, some crawled, others gathered amputated limbs and eyes and tails—but they all, every single one of them that wasn't blown to smithereens, survived the explosion.

Covie took a breath, steeling herself for Tom's reaction to what she was about to suggest. "Maybe we should move."

He rubbed his eyes and sighed. "Where would we go, Cove?"

"I don't know . . . the country? Somewhere we can get away from the larger concentration of plush infections and gang attacks—the killings." She shuddered as it sunk in how close she and Emily had come to being victims today.

"The city is just as safe as the country. Safer, in fact, with the people Tippy Toys has patrolling our neighborhood day and night. They're very efficient at blowing the infected plush to oblivion."

Covie folded her arms with a scowl. "Yeah, that really helped today when your daughter and I were attacked at an abandoned gas station!"

Tom stood and turned to face her. His face softened when he saw the tears in her eyes, and he pulled her into a hug. "I'm sorry. I know that must have been terrifying for both of you. But this just makes it even more important that we stay here, that I keep my job. Keep working on a cure." He pulled away to look at her with a wry smile. "And the money is nice. What would you and Em do if you couldn't go shopping several times a week?"

"I don't care about the money." She shook her head. She didn't have the energy for this. "I'm tired. I'm going to go to bed. How much longer are you going to be?"

He pulled her into another hug. "I don't know. I won't be able to sleep until I figure out this iteration of the formula I've been working on." He pointed to an open notebook with figures and numbers that were hieroglyphics to Covie. "I'll be up in a bit." He gave her a quick kiss on the lips.

* * *

"Cove. Covie?" Tom touched her shoulder.

She grumbled something even she wasn't sure made sense and rolled over.

"If you're going to work today, you'd better get up. Don't you have a client meeting you at the gym this morning?"

From under the covers, she mumbled, "I'm not feeling so great."

"I'm sorry you aren't feeling well. Your voice sounds weird. I'll leave breakfast for you and call the gym to let them know you won't be in. Maybe that new trainer can help out with your clients today." He paused, probably waiting for a comment from her, knowing she hated to leave her clients with another trainer. When she didn't respond, he said, "I'll get Em ready for school. You just get some rest."

Covie grunted, "Thanks," and fell back to sleep.

* * *

Covie's eyes fluttered open, and she scrambled to throw the heavy covers off her head before she suffocated. She blinked, trying to focus on the clock sitting on the nightstand next to her—10:52. She sat up with a start, panicking for a moment before remembering that Tom had taken care of everything this morning. At least she didn't feel lousy like earlier. She still felt like something was off, but she couldn't specify exactly what.

Tossing the covers the rest of the way off, Covie swung her feet over the side of the bed. They dangled instead of touching the floor beneath her. "What in the world?" Had Tom raised the bed for some reason? She scooted to

17

the edge and stuck her feet in her slippers before standing. Her pajama bottoms slid from her waist to the floor. She grabbed the waistband of her underwear, which were also loose, preventing them from sliding down to meet her PJs, which now pooled around her ankles.

Weird. Something must have happened with the laundry, causing stuff to stretch overnight. She bent over and pulled her bottoms back up, holding them at the waist, along with her underwear, under the now dress-length pajama top. The neck slid over her shoulder, and she shoved it back up as she started to walk, stumbling as her feet pulled out of her slippers. She staggered to the bathroom on bare feet, wondering groggily what happened to her clothes. She headed straight for the toilet, eyes squeezed shut as she yawned before sitting to do her morning business.

After flushing, she dragged herself over to the sink to wash her hands, the pajama bottoms falling back to the floor when she let go of them. Turning the water on, she glanced in the mirror and did a double take so fast, her neck popped with the motion. "Ahhh!" Covie screamed.

Staring back at her, eyes wide with bewilderment, was her eleven-year-old self.

CHAPTER

Impossible! Covie rubbed her eyes and looked again. She opened her mouth, stuck her tongue out, pulled at her nose, pushed her cheeks. The juvenile in the mirror copied her every move. She touched her face, squishing the smooth young skin in different directions as she leaned closer to the mirror, her heart rate increasing exponentially with every passing second. Covie smoothed her long brown hair and took a deep breath.

She looked down and screamed again, only this time it stuck in her throat and came out as more of a squeal. A preteen, girly squeal. She slapped her hands against her flat chest. "Where are my boobs?!"

The water continued to run in the sink. She'd forgotten all about hygiene. She raised her left arm and bent it, tightening what used to be a toned bicep. She touched and squeezed it with her right hand, her mind spinning out of control. "Skinny. It's skinny. All the years of working out . . . just gone."

Her eyes trailed down to the sagging underwear, her

stomach flipping like a cheerleader at homecoming. "My hips. My curves are gone. I look like a boy!"

Gripping the bathroom counter with trembling hands—tiny trembling hands—Covie shouted to the empty house, "What happened? How will I explain this to people?" She shook her head. "How do I explain this to myself?"

My life is over!

Am I going to have to relive my childhood?

Bile shot up into her throat. *Will I have to go through puberty again?!*

Covie grabbed her hair with both hands and held her breath, trying not to scream. Trying not to cry. She untangled her fingers from her hair and exhaled slowly. "Get it together, Covie White. Your mama raised you better than this. Just because you're a child on the outside doesn't mean you have to act like one."

After a few more calming breaths—thank you, yoga— she turned off the running water and grabbed her medication vial out of the cabinet, remembering what Tom had said about it last night. She turned the bottle so the label faced her. Phyzcoxin by SynthNA. She pulled her bottoms up and held them there with one hand, carrying the vial in the other as she shuffled to her home office.

She remained standing as she opened up a search engine on her laptop and typed "Phyzcoxin" into the search bar, quickly scanning the articles. All the links were highlighted from her previous searches years ago. She had read everything about Phyzcoxin and none of the side effects were reverse aging. She scrolled frantically while she combed her long brown hair with splayed fingers. The searches were a dead end, and she found nothing about her strange predicament.

A SynthNA pamphlet lay right next to her laptop on

the desk. She typed "SynthNA" into the search engine and clicked on the "Side Effects" tab when it pulled up. Covie's stomach growled, and her feet were getting cold standing barefoot on the hardwood floor. She grabbed her laptop and detoured through the kitchen to grab the toast and orange juice her husband had left for her before going to her room so she could sit on her bed while she researched. She had to balance the small plate and glass on top of her closed laptop so she could carry it with one hand while holding her pants up with the other. Her hand still hurt from the stupid exploding panda.

She set the food on her nightstand and climbed into her bed with the laptop, flipping it open when she got settled. Grabbing the toast from next to her, she read through the listed known side effects—none of which said anything about waking up in the body of a child.

Brushing crumbs off the sheets, Covie wondered if this ridiculous body swap came from whatever happened when she got burned, or zapped, by the panda from the claw machine. She stared at her small hand. "You'd think that at the very least, I'd get relief from this burn in exchange for all the inconvenience of being forced into the body of an eleven-year-old!" She shook her head—partly at the way she was talking to herself out loud and partly at the absurdity of the whole situation.

Covie closed the laptop and flopped back onto her pillow, covering her eyes with her arm. What was she going to do? No one could see her like this. She couldn't even go pick up Emily from school. Emily! She shot up and looked at the alarm clock. Relief flooded her chest. It was barely past noon.

Making a decision, Covie grabbed her phone, dialed her mom's number, and put it on speaker.

"Hey, Covie," her mom answered.

"Hey, Mom. I need a favor."

"Are you okay? You sound funny."

Crap! Covie cleared her throat and tried to deepen her voice to sound more like an adult. "I'm okay, I'm just standing kind of far from my phone. Sorry."

"Okay . . . what do you need?" The lilt in her mom's voice told Covie she wasn't completely buying her act.

"Can you please pick Emily up from school and drop her at home when Tom gets off?" Her mind reeled, trying to think of a good reason why she might be gone, not just today, but for . . . a while.

"Of course. Maybe Em and I will go get some ice cream." Her mom paused. Covie pictured her biting her thumbnail like she always did when something bothered her. "Covie . . . are you sure you're okay?"

She looked down at the SynthNA pamphlet she'd brought into her room with her laptop. "Actually, no. I'm having some strange side effects from my injections, and the company that makes the medication wants me to check into their hospital and . . . quarantine. I'm not sure how long I'll be there. They, uh, they want to run some tests."

Covie added the "quarantine" part so her family couldn't come visit while she was in the "hospital." She was pretty good at this—making stuff up on the fly. Maybe she should go on that game show where the contestants had to figure out which person was lying.

"Well okay, dear." Her mom sounded a little worried. "Please call if you need anything else."

After ending the call to her mom, she dialed Tom. Thankfully, he was too distracted to notice anything amiss with her newly immature voice. She gave him the same story and told him she'd be in touch as soon as she could.

"Cove," he said, "I was already around you last night. There's no reason to quarantine from me. I'll reschedule my meetings and meet you there."

"No, Tom." Covie bit her lip. "It's not like that, I just . . . it's their policy. They won't let you in anyway. It'll be an epic waste of your time. And you need to be there for Emily."

"There's no changing your mind?" Tom sighed.

"No."

"Okay, then. What symptoms do I need to be looking out for in Emily and me?"

"None, this only affects people taking the Phyzcoxin. I gotta go."

Covie hung up the phone before she had to make up any more lies.

CHAPTER SIX

With her daughter's closet doors spread wide open, Covie thought, *It's a good thing I buy Emily such cute clothes.* There was no way she was going to fit into any of her own clothing—unless she wanted to wear a shirt as a dress that would hang off her shoulders eighties style. But Emily's clothes would fit her.

After looking for several minutes, she decided on a pair of purple leggings under some denim shorts, a multicolored T-shirt, and a cropped puffy white vest that sparkled in the right light. She slipped on a pair of chunky-soled boots that Emily never wore.

Covie was going to figure this out and get her toned, athletic, C-cup breasted adult body back! She grabbed her purse and keys and headed into the garage. As she made her way to her car, she spotted a machete that had been on the shelf for at least a couple of years. She dragged a folding chair over, climbed up, and grabbed the weapon—the state of the world required such forethought.

As she climbed into the driver's seat, she realized a problem. She couldn't see over the steering wheel. With a growl of frustration, Covie ran to the backyard and grabbed a cushion off one of the deck chairs to boost her a little higher.

If she moved the seat forward almost as far as it would go, she could reach the gas and brake pedals with the ball of her boot-clad foot while sitting on the cushion. She started the car, slipped her fashion sunglasses on, and backed out—thanking the heavens for the invention of backup cameras.

She drove toward the Stop a Sec, wanting to examine the claw machine. It had to be either that machine or the Phyzcoxin injections that had caused her predicament, and she was going to get to the bottom of it. She parked near the front of the store and sat for a minute, staring at the broken windows and the propped-open door. She looked around the area from inside the car, peering into the bushes the plush had appeared from the night before. They seemed to all be gone. Plush stuffing and body parts littered the area; the frenzy must have continued for a while after she and Emily escaped.

Machete gripped tightly in her hand, she opened the car door and slid out, keeping an eye on her surroundings as she inched toward the gas station store. The shattered glass door lay broken off its hinges. Covie peered inside. The TV that had been broadcasting the news the night before now lay in pieces, face down on the floor. A chunk of drywall lay next to it, yanked out where the plug and cables had been ripped from the wall.

She stepped inside. A couple of tiny three-inch plush-ies hanging on an overturned keychain rack dragged themselves out from under its weight, growling at Covie. She jumped back, holding the machete out in front of her. Her fear turned to amusement for a moment as the little plushies struggled to reach her, trapped by the keychains attached to them on one end and the rack on the other. Two of the growling plush—an elephant and a sloth—thrashed around with enough vigor to free themselves, landing on the floor. They rushed toward her and she screamed, chopping down on the elephant with the machete and stomping the sloth with the sole of her daughter's chunky boot.

Covie rushed to the side of the store, toward the claw machine, and stopped with a skid. The machine was gone. A square of lint and dust was the only thing remaining to show where it had once been. She dropped her arms to her sides, still gripping the machete in one hand, as horror engulfed her, squeezing the breath out of her lungs. The claw machine was gone. What if it had been the only thing that would put her right again?

The now-headless elephant slammed up against the back of her boot, kicking at her Achilles tendon through the faux leather material. Covie kicked her foot and sent the tiny plush flying into an overturned shelf. A scratching, dragging sound caught her attention, and she turned to glare at the flattened sloth as it inched its way toward her, pulling itself and the metal keychain along with one arm.

With one last look at the empty spot where the claw machine had been only yesterday, where this whole blasted mess had begun, Covie stomped to the exit, kicking the sloth back to the rack from where it had crawled—from where other tiny plush keychains growled and flailed and gnashed their felt teeth.

Covie climbed back into her car and up onto the seat cushion/booster seat, locked the doors, and let her tears flow. "What in the world am I going to do now?" She stared at the steering wheel as if waiting for it to answer her. When it didn't offer even a peep of a response, she slammed her eleven-year-old-sized fists into it until her knuckles hurt.

"I need coffee." She wiped her face clean of tears and started the car.

CHAPTER SEVEN

The barista put her hands on her hips and looked behind Covie, probably to see if there was a parent accompanying the child. "Aren't you a little young to be wandering around by yourself?"

Covie huffed out a breath. "Look, my mom is just down the block buying me a birthday present. She told me to come in here and chill while she shops." She held up her credit card. "She even gave me one of the credit cards to pay with."

The twenty-something girl behind the counter shrugged. "Okay, what can I get you?"

Covie eased the tightness building in her neck and shoulders by rolling her head from side to side and back and forth. "I'll have a skim-milk caramel latte macchiato. Medium, please." It was her favorite drink, even though the caramel added too many calories, and she didn't let herself order it often. She looked down at her scrawny legs and thin wrists. Calories hardly mattered at the moment. She never thought she'd be wanting those calories to matter.

She resolved to talk to Tom when he got home that night. He needed to know what happened to her. He was the scientist, after all, and she knew he could figure it out and get her back to normal. She looked down at her tiny legs. He just had to, because she didn't want to consider what her life would be like if he couldn't.

The girl took Covie's credit card and inserted it into the register. "You know, coffee will stunt your growth," she quipped as she handed it back to her with the receipt.

Covie rolled her eyes and grabbed the proffered card and slip of paper before finding a table tucked off in a corner. She sat, folded her arms on top of the inlaid tile, and laid her head in her arms. She'd really thought that going back to the claw machine would fix everything. But with it gone, now what could she do? She'd thought that she just needed to do something simple—like repeat her actions from yesterday, maybe nab the walrus Emily had wanted so badly.

"Covie!" the barista yelled.

She retrieved her coffee and sat back in the corner. What was she going to do? She sipped her latte, the warm drink soothing her frazzled nerves at least for a moment. Her eyes wandered around the small coffee shop, past the TV with the closed-captions that silently narrated some rom-com movie from the last decade. Her gaze was drawn back to it when a colorful symbol from the news station covered the screen, the words "Breaking News" emblazoned across the middle.

A reporter with a fake tan came on, brows knit together in a serious look. Covie silently read the words scrolling across the bottom of the screen.

"Five scientists from the Safe Stuffing company— Tippy Toys Inc.—were kidnapped from the company's headquarters about an hour ago."

Covie stood, staring hard at the TV.

"There has been no ransom demanded as of yet and the company has refused to comment on the abductions."

Leaning forward over the table, she whispered, "Names, you dimwitted lobster. What are the scientists' names?"

As if answering her plea, the words scrolling across the screen said, "The five scientists have been identified as Chad Connelly . . ."

Oh no. Chad was her best friend's husband.

"Tom White . . ."

"No!" Covie yelled. She bumped the table and knocked her drink to the floor. It splattered in a five-foot radius, droplets hitting anyone standing nearby.

She ignored the comments being flung at her and fished her phone from her purse. She called Tom's phone and pressed hers against her ear, looking away from the glaring customers. She was going to come clean about what happened with her this morning when he picked up. With each unanswered ring, her heart pounded harder and faster. The few sips she'd taken of her drink hardened into rocks in her stomach. "Please, babe. Please answer . . ."

"This is Tom, leave a message." *Beep*

Gripping her phone in a tight fist, she left a message. "Tom! Where are you?! Is it true? What's happening?! We just talked less than an hour ago!"

Everyone in the shop was looking at her. Covie scowled and flapped her hand at them, wanting them to just leave her alone. She tried texting Tom.

What is going on!! Are you safe??? Call me!!

No reply.

She slammed her phone on the table. The girl working the counter came over and started mopping up her mess. Covie turned her back to her and picked her phone up again to call her mom. "Mom? Is Emily okay?"

"Yes, dear, she's fine. I just picked her up, why?"

"Haven't you seen the news?" Covie took a breath to tone down the hysteria making her little-girl voice even higher pitched. She tried to make it sound older. "Mom, Tom's been kidnapped."

"What? By who?"

"I don't know, Mom! I just saw it on the news." She rubbed her forehead. "It has to be the plush, one of the gangs. There have been more attacks around here the last few days."

"Oh, I hope not," her mom said. "I did hear that some of the horrible plush gangs are trying to move in and take over this area, but I thought it was just Phyllis trying to start more gossip!"

"It's true. They're getting bolder." Covie looked out the window, expecting to see a gang of the monsters converging on the coffee shop. But the street out front was mostly empty, not a plush in sight. "Mom, stay with Emily, please. I'm going to go to the police station."

"Can you just leave the hospital?"

Oops. She forgot about her lie. "I suppose not. But I'd better at least call the police. I need to find out what's going on with my husb—" Covie glanced up at the people watching her and remembered she was in a child's body. "With Tom."

"Don't worry about Emily, honey. I'll take care of her," her mom said. "Let me know what you find out, please."

"Thanks, Mom. Bye." Covie shoved her phone in her purse and looped the strap around her shoulder. She was going down to the police station. She pulled her keys half-way out of her purse before noticing the silence in the crowded shop. She dropped them back in before looking up at the staring adults. She couldn't go to the police station. She was an eleven-year-old, at least on the outside, and that would be weird.

"Is everything all right, sweetheart?" a grandmotherly woman with blue hair asked.

"Umm. Yes, I . . . I just need to go meet my mom at her car." She looked over at the girl cleaning up her spilled coffee. "I'm sorry."

She hurried to her car, parked around the corner out of sight of anyone who may have been looking out the windows of the businesses nearby, and called her best friend.

Charlotte answered on the first ring. "Covie! Did you hear? What are we going to do? Who could have done this?" She sniffed. Her voice was high and shaky, so maybe Covie's wouldn't sound so out of the ordinary considering the circumstances.

"I heard. I don't know what to do. Do you think it's a plush gang that has them? Have you heard anything from the police or the company?"

"I haven't heard a word from anyone. I can't believe they let us find out from the TV!"

Covie started her car and pulled onto the street. "I'm going home right now. I'm going to call the police and see what they know."

CHAPTER EIGHT

Covie rushed into the house before the garage door had even halfway shut. She threw her purse on the counter and pulled out her phone again, dialing the police station.

"Dia Metro City Police, Officer McDonald speaking," a harried-sounding man answered.

Crap. What was she going to say? She should have thought this out a little better before calling. "I'm Tom White's . . . daughter. Can you please tell me what's going on? Who kidnapped him? What are you doing to try to find him?"

The officer sighed. "Look, little girl, kids should not be calling the police. Let the grown-ups take care of things." He hung up.

No one would take her seriously in her current state.

She'd just have to go find her husband herself, and she planned on starting at Tippy Toys headquarters. She grabbed a sparkly backpack out of the coat closet and stuffed an extra set of clothes, protein bars, and dried fruit into it. She entered Tom's home office and prayed she'd find what she was looking for. She nearly wept when she found it in the top drawer of his desk. Covie shoved the extra key card into an outside pocket of the backpack, hoping it would still work to gain entrance into the Tippy Toys building.

The machete went into another outside pocket, the handle sticking out for easy access. Remembering some camping stuff stowed away in the garage, she went out there and added a flashlight, a canteen, a rain poncho, some freeze-dried food, and anything else she found that would fit in the backpack and might be useful.

Back inside, she flopped onto the couch. She had too much adrenaline to rest, but knew she would have to wait until dark to go to Tippy Toys. She checked her phone, hoping to see a message from Tom.

Nothing.

Her heart leapt into her throat at a loud knock on the front door. Covie got up and peered out the window. It was Charlotte. Her best friend lived just down the street—of course she'd come over during such a time of crisis. Covie didn't know what to do. Should she answer the door and let Charlotte in on the incredible shrink-ing-body fiasco? Would she freak out?

Covie shook her head. She'd known Charlotte for years. They'd shared innumerable secrets and experiences together. If she should tell anyone about this, it should be her.

Steeling herself for the inevitable freakout, Covie opened the door and ushered Charlotte in.

"Who are you and what are you doing in Cove and Tom's house?!"

Covie shut the door. "Char, come sit down. Let me expl—"

"How do you know my name? Where are Cove and

Emily?" Char waved her hands around. "Where are your parents, young lady?"

"Char, please," Covie begged.

Charlotte shook her head. "Oh no. Don't 'Char' me like you know me, kid. I'm going to call the police. There are homeless shelters and foster homes for kids like you. There's no need to squat in someone else's house." She reached for her phone in her back pocket.

"Charlotte! Don't!" Covie grabbed the phone from her. "It's me! Cove! Just let me explain."

"Give that back." Char held her hand out, but hesitated when she looked closer at Covie.

"I swear, it's me, Char." How could she convince her? She'd have to do something drastic. "Remember our girls' trip to Vegas? That bachelorette party?"

Charlotte's eyes widened, and she covered her mouth with her hand.

Covie rushed to finish before her friend stopped her. "We partied till the middle of the night, and when we woke up . . . the groom was in bed with us. Neither of us could remember what happened, but we swore to never tell another soul."

"And those two are still happily married. I need to sit down." Char shuffled to the couch, glancing at Covie every couple of steps.

"Do you believe me now?" Covie asked after they'd sat down.

Char nodded, then shook her head, then nodded again. "I guess I have to, but what the heck happened?"

"I wish I knew." Covie explained to her about the claw machine and the panda that burned her. She showed Char her hand, still raw and sore.

"That's just . . ." Char shook her head. "Crazy, Covie."

"Yeah. I know."

"What are you going to do? Who else knows?"

"No one else knows. I have to find Tom."

Char held her hand. "Let the police handle it, Covie. It's too dangerous."

"I can't. I can't wait for them. I need to find my husband and figure out what made me young again."

Her friend sighed. "How can I help?"

Relief washed over Covie. Char really was her best friend. "Please help my mom take care of Emily. And cover for me." She told her the cover story about Phyzcoxin that she'd come up with on the fly.

"Okay. I will. But, Cove, doing this by yourself is a bad idea." She gestured at the sequined backpack where the machete stuck out. "It's dangerous."

"I know. But I have to find Tom. And I have to find that claw machine."

"How do you know the two things are even connected?"

Covie shrugged. "Call it a hunch. Tom and the Biotoy division he just got moved to have been experimenting, trying to find a cure for this crazy plushdemic. It's controversial and top secret." She leaned forward, closer to her friend. "It's like a mother's instinct. Or a wife's instinct, I don't know. It just feels like Biotoy, the kidnapping, and"—Covie fluttered her hands from her head to her knees—"*this* are connected."

"Okay," Char said, "I'll help with Emily, and I'll keep your mom from asking too many questions if I can."

"Thank you, Charlotte." Covie hugged her friend. "I can do this. I'll keep you updated."

CHAPTER NINE

As darkness fell, Covie headed to Tippy Toys headquarters in the city. The building was deserted, dark except for the emergency lights they always left on after hours. Police tape surrounded the entrance. Covie drove around back to employee parking. She grabbed the key card, the sparkly backpack, and her purse, then ducked under the police tape. She looked around before hurrying to the doors, where a large chain was looped through the handles and fastened with a padlock.

Covie smiled and dropped her purse to the ground, crouching down to rummage through it. Being the daughter of a locksmith had come in handy throughout her life, but tonight more than ever. "Ha!" she whisper-yelled as she found the small leather case holding a set of lock-picking tools she'd carried with her ever since her father had given it to her for her sixteenth birthday. She looked around one more time to ensure she was alone, then set to work picking the lock.

It was old and only took her a few minutes to open. She stuffed it and the chain under a bush and used Tom's key card to enter the building. Flicking the flashlight from her pack to life, she entered his office down the hall from the Biotoy laboratory. She swept the room with the cone of light. Everything seemed to be in place. She didn't know how or where the kidnapping had taken place, but there was no sign of a struggle in here.

She moved to the desk and sat in his chair, her feet dangling above the ground. She opened each drawer—looking in every folder, notebook, or envelope she came across—hoping to find any information about Tom's disappearance or who might have had a motive to take him. And looking for anything that might show the locations of the company's claw machines.

Pressure built behind her eyes as she slammed the last drawer shut. She'd found nothing useful. Nothing. She dropped her head into her hands and released the flood of tears she'd been holding back. She kicked the metal trash can under the desk and railed in the silence. "I want my husband back! I want to be forty again! How can I be a mom to Emily in this stupid child body?!" She looked up at the ceiling. "Tom, where are you? I need you. Em needs her daddy." She wouldn't let herself consider that Tom might be hurt, or worse.

Covie allowed herself a few more minutes of crying, then took a deep breath and wiped her face on the sleeve of her daughter's T-shirt. What next? She used her phone to look up the latest news story on the kidnappings, finding no new information since the last time she'd checked. But she wasn't searching for new information. She scrolled through the story to where the names of the missing scientists were listed. She recognized a name from the doorplate on the office across the hall from Tom's and went there to search next.

Nothing.

Again.

Maybe this all had something to do with the new project Tom was working on. The cure to the plushdemic. A thought struck Covie like a bolt of lightning—who on Earth would *not* want a cure to be found for the infected plush? The infected plush, of course. The thought of becoming nothing but inanimate playthings again must terrify them.

Covie made her way to the new Biotoy wing of the building, where Tom and his team had been working on a cure. She swiped his card and one set of doors whooshed open into an anteroom, closing behind her when she stepped in. Fans kicked on for about ten seconds before the second set of doors opened, letting her into the lab.

"Wow."

It was huge. Lab equipment and computers covered almost every surface. Large glass-doored refrigerators full of racks of vials lined one wall. Covie walked down the aisle between the equipment-laden countertops and a wall of evenly spaced doors. At each corner of the counter was a modular lab station, likely one for each scientist. She came to Tom's station—a family photo with the three of them smiling at the camera was tacked to a small corkboard in one of the cubby-like spaces. His station was tidy, his microscope covered and his computer turned off.

A nameplate that said "Tom White, PhD" marked the door to his lab office. Covie entered and searched his mostly empty desk. He'd only been using this office for a couple of weeks. In the top drawer, she found a professional-looking leatherbound journal and, too antsy to sit, she leaned over the desk as she opened it and read Tom's precise handwriting.

Hypothesis:
It has become more and more evident that the key

to finding a cure to this pandemic/plushdemic is finding Plush Zero—the first plush to become infected. We've looked at other avenues, and all other leads will take too long. Plush Zero—finding the source—is the fastest way to find a cure.

Covie skipped over the scientific gobbledygook that read like a foreign language to her and flipped to the next page. Tom had sketched out a pedigree chart of sorts, working backward to figure out where the infection had started. The space labeled "Plush Zero" was blank. But . . . the second slot, just under Plush Zero, had a name: *WINDOW.*

She pulled her phone out and snapped a picture of the chart. This Window plush would have to lead her to Plush Zero. And Plush Zero would have to have the answers. Answers for Tom and the other scientists, and answers for Covie on how to get her grown-up body back.

CHAPTER TEN

Covie grinned and a rush of adrenaline shot through her veins. She had a plan—find Window and force the plush to tell her who Plush Zero was and where to find him. Figuring the journal might come in handy, she put it in her backpack and made her way to the employee entrance in the back of the building.

A security guard stepped out from a dark intersecting hallway, stopping Covie's heart with his abrupt and unexpected appearance. Her presence had a similar effect on him, exhibited by his full-body flinch and the rapid draining of color from his face. "What are you doing in here?" His stern voice belied his surprise at seeing her.

Shoot. "Umm . . . I was supposed to meet my big sister here, but I can't find her."

The guard narrowed his eyes at her. "How did you get in the building? It's all locked up. I checked all the doors an hour ago."

She shrugged, channeling her inner tween to match the outer version.

Shaking his head, the guard wagged his finger at her.

"It's dangerous to be here, young lady. A bunch of scientists were kidnapped from this building today, ya know."

She, in fact, did know. That's why she was here. "Ohh . . . that's scary," she said. "It's a good thing you're here to keep an eye on things."

The guard straightened up and put his hands on his hips above his duty belt. "Yep. If I'd been here earlier, I would have stopped those kidnappers."

Covie fought the eye roll that wanted so badly to surface. "Hey, do you know anything about Plush Zero?" she asked.

"Plush Zero?" The furrow in his brow deepened. "No, can't say that I do."

It was worth a try. "What about a plush named Window? Do you know anything about him?"

He held up a hand, palm facing her. "Oh, I can't really talk about that."

Trying to copy her daughter's expression when she was trying to talk her or Tom into something, Covie widened her eyes and blinked, then smiled up at the guard. "Please tell me, Officer. I promise I won't rat you out." *Do kids even say that anymore?* she wondered.

The lines on his face softened and he relaxed his stance and smiled. "Well . . . you are just a kid. I suppose it wouldn't hurt to tell you a little."

Covie bounced on her toes and clapped, hoping to encourage the man to spill his guts.

He leaned closer and lowered his voice conspiratorially. "I overheard Ralph, the daytime guard, say that Window is an infamous mobster plush that runs the south side of the city. Word among the security guards here is that *he* was the one who kidnapped the scientists."

That lucky little piece of intel was just what she needed. She brushed her hair out of her face and smiled.

"Thank you, Officer. I'd better be going, now. Maybe my sister is waiting for me outside."

The guard frowned. "Be careful. It's dangerous out there."

"I will. Promise." She turned toward the exit at the end of the hallway.

"Hey! Stop! What's that in your backpack?" He pointed with a beefy index finger.

She stopped and twisted slowly back toward him, wondering how he could possibly know about the journal she'd taken from Tom's Biotoy office. "What?" She put all the innocence she could muster into that one word.

He pointed at the machete handle sticking out of the side pocket.

Glancing from the handle back to the guard, she held his gaze as she said, "It's for protection. It's dangerous out there, remember?" She smiled.

CHAPTER ELEVEN

The security guard had been right about at least one thing: It *was* dangerous out there. Covie drove around for a while, unsure what to do or where to go. When she could no longer keep her eyes open, she pulled over beneath a dark overpass and crawled in the back seat to get some sleep.

It felt like she'd just fallen asleep when a noise woke her up. She froze, listening.

"Got it!" a man's voice said.

Light from a flashlight flickered on the window next to the driver's seat, where a man wearing dark clothes and a knit beanie slid a slim-jim tool out of the door.

Covie shot up and ripped the machete out of her backpack and out of its sheath.

The man opened the door and unlocked the others with the push of a button, then shined his light into the back seat. "Well, well, well, look what we have here."

The sliminess of his voice sent a shudder down Covie's back as she gripped the knife tighter.

"Donny, looky here. It's our lucky night. A car *and* a little girl to . . . play with."

"Leave me alone!" Covie yelled, pointing the machete at the creepy guy.

The back passenger door swung open and Donny, greasy-haired and with some kind of neck tattoo, grinned widely, showing multiple gaps where teeth should have been. "She's a cute one." He licked his lips. "I get to go first this time while you hold the flashlight."

"Ah, man. I like to deflower these young ones." The guy with the beanie climbed into the front, facing backward, and leaned over the seat, shining the light in Covie's eyes. "But I like to watch, too."

"Leave me alone. I'm warning you," Covie seethed through a clenched jaw. These two disgusting perverts made her blood boil.

Donny unzipped his pants and let them drop to his knees. "Whatchya gonna do with that knife, little girl?" He lunged for her and grabbed her leg, digging his filthy fingernails into her skin.

Covie swung the machete at the sleazeball, swiping the blade cleanly across his throat. Warm blood sprayed her face as Donny tried to scream, only able to gurgle. He sat up and slapped both hands to his neck as blood poured between his fingers and color faded from his skin.

"Donny!" the dying man's partner shouted, reaching for him.

Donny's eyes rolled back and he slumped to the seat, then slid out of the car to the ground, the gasping, gurgling sounds becoming less frequent.

"You killed Donny!" The remaining molester dove over the seat and grabbed Covie around the throat, knocking the machete out of her hand.

She clutched at his strong fingers with both her hands, slippery with blood. Her tiny child's hands couldn't peel his fingers away from her throat. She thrashed around as his grip tightened, unable to get any air in.

The man propelled himself the rest of the way over the seat, now fully in the back of the car with Covie. She pounded on his arms and face, fear racing through her as her lungs burned with the need for oxygen.

He loosened his grip and removed one hand from her throat, slapping her across the face. She ignored the sting as she gasped in a breath.

"I'm gonna kill ya for what ya did to Donny, girl." He pushed her down onto the seat and arranged himself above her. "But first," he grunted as he reached to unbutton his jeans with his free hand, "I'm gonna have some fun with ya."

Covie twisted and turned under his grip on her throat and the weight of him pressing down on her. Her hand brushed against something hard on the floor. The machete! She found the handle and gripped it with all her might.

The man raised up and reached for the waist of her shorts. With a primal scream, Covie plunged the machete into his thigh, then yanked it out for another strike as the man's blood mingled with that of his now-dead friend.

Before Covie could swing the blade again, the man, screaming curses at her, flung himself out of the car, landing on top of dead Donny. As he struggled to stand, Covie slammed the door and scrambled to the front seat to hit the lock button, locking all four doors at once.

A bloody hand slapped against the rear passenger window as the man gained his feet, still flinging curses at her. She started the car and put it in gear, squealing the tires as she pulled back onto the deserted street. Anger coursed through her. Animals like that man didn't deserve to live.

Covie cranked the wheel, spinning the car around so it was aimed at the bleeding miscreant. His eyes widened as she hit the gas, and he turned and ran with a limp, throwing himself into the ditch at the side of the road.

She drove to a more populated area, hyperventilating as the reality of what just happened set in. She parked at the back of a well-lit parking lot, tears welling up in her eyes. She calmed her breathing and wiped her cheeks. Then she huddled in her car until morning came, too afraid to sleep. There was no going back from this now.

CHAPTER TWELVE

Just before dawn, Covie drove to a mostly deserted convenience store she knew had a restroom with the entrance on the outside. She parked right next to the women's bathroom and took her backpack in with her. Using a pile of wet paper towels, she cleaned the blood off herself as well as she could in the small, dirty restroom. She rinsed her long brown hair out in the nasty sink, watching in sort of a trance as the red-tinted water slowly circled the drain.

She'd killed a man—at least one man. Who knew if the other one was still alive. She thought of her own daughter's safety and hoped he wasn't. Covie wrapped her arms around herself, goose bumps popping out on her flesh.

Vomit erupted from her throat without warning, splashing into the sink and up onto the mirror. This was followed by a couple of episodes of dry heaving, with nothing left in her stomach to expel.

"Get a grip, Covie," she whispered to her dim reflection in the grimy mirror as she clutched the sides of the sink. "It was self-defense . . . and those men deserved what they got." She closed her eyes and breathed slowly, in and out, until the nausea subsided.

A horizontal gash under her left eye started to bleed. She retrieved the roll of duct tape from her backpack. Ripping an inch piece off and then ripping that piece in half, she wiped the blood from the wound and stuck the makeshift Band-Aid to her cheekbone.

She rinsed out her mouth, then hurried to change into the spare outfit she'd packed in the backpack. After wiping dried blood splatter and wet vomit off her boots, Covie left the bathroom, trying not to feel guilty for leaving it dirtier than it had already been.

Finding the plush mob boss, Window, was what she needed to do now. He could lead her to Plush Zero, her kidnapped husband and his colleagues, and possibly to where all the claw machines were. Covie was fairly certain about the first two, and mostly just hopeful for the last one. She didn't know why, but her instincts just told her the plush were behind what had happened with the panda.

The Tippy Toys security guard had said Window ran the south side of the city, so that's where she headed, not knowing how to find him when she got there.

Covie parked curbside on a dilapidated block and ate a protein bar and some dried fruit while she watched out her tinted windows. There didn't seem to be any people there; the plush had taken over the whole area.

A raccoon plush staggered into an alley, a near-empty bottle of whiskey clasped in its paw.

"I ain't no trash panda!" the raccoon slurred. "I'm a bandit and I like it that way. Trash panda . . ." It bent over and picked up a half-eaten hot dog smashed near a puddle. It gobbled down the dog first, then scooped the soggy bun up and slurped it down next. A burp from the disgusting plush echoed off the walls of the alley.

The thing tried to get up, but it fell, passing out on its face just as the shadows of the alley enveloped it. The bottle rolled out onto the sidewalk, the sun glinting off the glass as its rays peeked around a cloud.

Covie watched for movement in the darkened alley as a plan formed in her mind. Seeing none, she peered around her, watching for an opportunity. A small gang of maimed plush of varying sizes—a llama, a leopard, and a frog—elbowed and punched each other as they made their way down the middle of the street. After they turned the corner, the path was clear. Covie shoved her phone, sunglasses, and keys into the backpack and stuffed her purse under the seat, taking the backpack—and machete—with her. With one more look around to ensure she wouldn't be spotted, she exited her car, locking it before softly shutting the door.

In the dark alley—the buildings to either side tall enough to block out the sun's light—she nudged the inebriated raccoon plush with her toe. It snorted and rolled over on its side. Perfect, it was the same size as Covie's new body and basically unconscious. She set the backpack down next to an overflowing dumpster and slipped the machete out of its sheath. Standing over the prostrate plushie, she closed her eyes, picturing Tom and Emily, reminding herself why she needed to do what she was about to do.

Stepping on the raccoon's head to stabilize it, she sliced across the back of its neck. The drunk plush barely even responded, just a grunt and a twitch of its tail. She set the machete next to her as she knelt beside the large stuffed animal. As she reached her hand into the plush's head, she regretted eating earlier. She buried her nose in her shoulder for a minute, trying to stifle the blood, booze, and BO overwhelming her senses.

She pulled out all the stuffing from the head, then the body and limbs—even the tail of the raccoon. She'd watched a documentary recently about a taxidermist who had inadvertently discovered that if you removed all the inner blood stuffing from the infected plushies, they didn't reanimate. It was the only way to completely kill them. She remembered the guy's warning, though—even with the outer skin separated from the inner plush, the materials were extremely contagious by contact and through the air. He'd cautioned that if there were any unanimated plush in the vicinity, they would become infected and animate. Covie wasn't too worried about that. Every plush in this neighborhood had likely already been infected.

When every scrap of bloody cotton had been pulled, scraped, and separated from the raccoon's "skin," Covie gathered up the slimy pile and stuffed it into the dumpster. Lastly, she cut out the plastic eyes, leaving holes in their place. Her arms and hands were slathered with dark red blood, strands of cotton fibers glued to her skin. Her fingernails were packed with the stuff. She grimaced. Now was not the time to be squeamish; what she was about to do would be the grossest, most disgusting thing she'd ever done.

She dug the roll of duct tape out of her backpack and ripped a piece off, sticking the end of it to the edge of the dumpster in preparation. She ripped a longer piece off and taped the machete's sheath to her right thigh, wrapping the tape around her leg several times, then cut a pocket-sized slit in the raccoon skin so she could get to it, before sliding the machete into place. She paused, thinking about what else she might need to reach in a hurry. She took her phone out of the backpack and shoved it in her back pocket, grabbed her sunglasses and balanced them on a rock, and then put the backpack on and slithered into the raccoon's skin, stretching the material where she'd slashed its neck, until she wore it like a mascot costume.

Determined to go all in, Covie slipped the disgusting empty head over her own, forcing herself to swallow down the bile rising in her throat as the repulsive stench engulfed her.

She taped the back of the neck where she'd sliced into it, knowing the maimed and pieced-together plush wouldn't think a thing about it, then put her sunglasses on to cover the eye holes she'd cut.

Covie was ready for Operation to Hell You Ride.

CHAPTER THIRTEEN

With a confident swagger, Covie stepped up to a plush cow half her size, one horn dangling in front of its face and a plastic bowl taped to its underside in place of the missing udder.

"Hey, cow!" She used her sternest mom voice. "Where's Window's hideout?"

The cow swung its head to look at her, its broken horn smacking it on the snout. "Why should I tell you, rodent?"

Covie was thrilled that her disguise seemed to be working, but she was in no mood to waste time arguing with a stupid animated plush cow. She pulled the machete out, pressing the tip against the cow's nose. "This is why."

The plush stepped back and Covie moved with it, the knife's point never losing contact with the faux leather nose.

"Tell me where Window's hideout is, or I'll gut you and stretch your stuffing from here to the north side of town."

Something like a wince passed over the cow's furry face. "Okay. Geez. Lower your . . . sword . . . thing, and I'll tell you."

Covie lowered it but kept a tight grip on the handle, thankful she'd chosen to wear a plush that had five fingers. "Spill it."

"Go down the alley between the First Choice Loan skyscraper and Sixes Casino. There's a door toward the back on the casino side. That's where Window's hideout is."

"See, that wasn't so hard, was it, Milky?" Covie stowed the machete back inside the plush skin suit and strode toward the First Choice skyscraper.

She retaped the machete to herself again before rounding the corner. Once finished with the concealment, she followed a furry frog through the door and did a quick scan of the room before blending in among the many plush mobsters. If her situation weren't so serious, she might have laughed at the absurdity of stuffed animals wearing suit vests and mobster hats, as some of them were. All thoughts of joviality left her as she noticed that many of the various types of plush had guns—either strapped to them or carried in their arms.

Clinking silverware and obnoxious slurping, snuffling, and chewing sounds turned Covie's attention to tables of varying sizes where plush sat or stood while they ate. She'd never really thought about the animated stuffed animals eating before—it just seemed so bizarre—but she supposed they were somehow organic now, and organic things needed nutrients.

Servers and patrons alike ignored her presence. She was just another plush to them. Thank heavens. Standing in a darkened corner, Covie surveyed the hideout, trying to figure out which one of them was Window—if any.

I probably should have found out what type of plush he is before coming here. She was annoyed with herself that she hadn't asked the security guard and frustrated with Tom for not writing it in his journal.

A raucous group of card-playing plush caught her attention. A rat slammed its cards down on the table and shouted, "Winner!"

The weasel sitting across from it jumped up on the table and got in the rat's face. "You dirty rat! You cheated! You and your kangaroo friend there!" It hopped to stand in front of the kangaroo. "Show me what's in your pouch, Sheila!"

Sheila kicked the table, sending the weasel, cards, coins, and drinks flying. "No one looks in my pouch, slimeball."

"Knock it off over there before I have Kong throw you losers out," said a large rooster plush with an eye patch. The feather in the hatband of its black fedora bounced with the movement of its head. "And clean up that mess!"

That must be Window. Covie took the opportunity to move closer to the rooster's table while the card players scrambled to clean up. She needed to be sure it was him.

"Hey, boss." A tailless skunk with a gun strapped to its side waltzed up to the rooster and nodded.

"Stinky," the rooster acknowledged.

Boss . . . that has to be him, right? She certainly hadn't pictured a rooster as a mob boss.

"Hi there, Window." A sultry-voiced pig with long eyelashes and lipstick, a safety pin holding her corkscrew tail in place, slid next to him. "Want some company?"

It's him. But I can't just stand here by myself listening to their conversation. It looks too suspicious. Covie looked around for some sort of cover. Her eyes landed on the bar, where a tray of drinks sat, waiting for a server.

She hustled over and stepped behind the bar, exuding

confidence that she belonged there. She grabbed an apron from a pile under the counter and tied it around her furry waist before lifting the tray of drinks. She missed her toned adult arms—not that the tray was all that heavy, but if she had to hold it for long, she had doubts her skinny arms could handle it.

Standing off at an angle to Window's table, she held the tray and listened to the conversation.

"So, boss," the skunk said, "the fellas are wondering what the plan is now that we got the scientists."

"Are 'the fellas' wondering?" Window pinned Stinky with his one eye.

"Well, yeah." The skunk shrugged. "Right, Legless?"

A big plush snake, the kind Covie had seen hanging from carnival tents as a prize, flicked its stub of a tongue. "Yessss. You sssaid you'd tell usss after we sssnatched them."

Window leaned back, resting his wings behind his head while the lipsticked pig rubbed his belly. "I did say that, didn't I?"

Covie leaned forward. She didn't want to miss a word of this "plan."

CHAPTER FOURTEEN

"A little to the right, sweetheart," Window said to the girlish pig. He looked around the table at his henchmen. "One: Now that we know the locations of all the claw machines—thank you, Poe, for locating those while the others were abducting the science guys"—he nodded at a stuffed raven standing on the table—"we can go to said locations and procure said claw machines to get the plush out."

She knew it! The infected plush *did* have something to do with those blasted machines. Covie had to roll her eyes at the rooster plush's attempt to sound intelligent.

The mob boss continued. "Two: Make a deal with those five scientists we now have in our little prison wing here—said deal being to give up the Safe Stuffing formula, or never leave this place alive."

Heat rushed to Covie's face and her grip tightened on the tray of drinks. How dare that little, smelly fowl puff threaten to kill her husband!

"Three: We"—he gestured to the crew around the table—"will reverse engineer said formula so we can animate the Safe Stuffing plush from the claw machines. Four: We will use these new recruits to take down Plush

Zero and his gang of ne'er-do-wells so *we* can be in charge of this whole city."

The tray was getting heavy. Covie's forearms ached from holding it.

"And five: This one may be out of order, but we shall see. If the scientists refuse to give up the formula, we kill them. Any questions?"

"Yeah, boss." The skunk rested its hand on its gun and grinned. "I got that last part. Just say the word."

The raven, Poe, dismissed Stinky with a roll of its black eyes, then turned to Window. "We found more booby-trapped claw machines this morning, boss, but they'd all been disarmed."

Stinky whipped his head around to stare at the raven. "Who woulda done that? Not that I'm complainin'—I was gettin' a little gun-shy when emptyin' 'em out. But why booby-trap 'em, then undo it?"

"The toy company disarmed them." Poe looked down his beak at the gun-toting skunk. "We saw a technician with their logo on his coveralls messing with one of them. But rest assured, they are not the ones who set the snares to begin with."

Window looked over his shoulder and spotted Covie in the plush raccoon skin. "Hey, you!" he shouted at her. "Why are you holding those drinks there . . ."

Oh crap! Thinking he'd caught her, she just shrugged, not knowing what else to do.

The mob boss continued. ". . . instead of putting them down in front of us?"

Covie freed the breath she'd held hostage in her lungs, stepped over to the table, and set the whole tray down.

The group of plush mobsters grabbed the drinks, except the snake, who slurped his by dunking his tongue into the glass. The drinks were chugged down before she'd even taken two steps away from them.

After the close call, Covie left the area and stood in a darkened corner, where she could observe the clientele but stay mostly unseen. As she watched the bizarre world of the animated plush, she tried to piece together everything she knew and everything she'd just heard. *My guess is it was Plush Zero that booby-trapped the claw machines to try to catch whoever's been cleaning them out and collecting all the plush. But all he caught was* me *when I touched that blasted tainted panda.* She shook her head, now even more convinced it was the panda incident that had caused her body to reverse age.

Covie perked up, narrowing her eyes as she focused on the back corner area. She wished she could take the sunglasses off—they made it really hard to see in the dim light—but that would give her away for sure. Moving out of the shadows and closer to the activity in the corner, she gasped when she recognized some of the little blue bears from the battle she'd fought at the gas station—where this had all begun. They were going in and out of a door.

She snuck back to the corner, trying not to look suspicious, and stood next to a tall dead plant until the last of the blue creatures disappeared through the door. Then she followed them. She wasn't sure why she felt compelled to do so—but if nothing else, she'd stomp a few of them until their stuffing was nothing but bloody mush for daring to try to attack her daughter.

The bears turned down a hallway to her left, and she took one angry step in their direction before realizing what lay down the hall in front of her. The narrow cement walkway was lined on either side with doors of thick bars, secured with padlocks. A jail. And Covie had left her lock-picking kit in her purse in the car.

Surveying her surroundings to make sure she was alone, she advanced toward the first cell and peered in. A single dull lightbulb lit the small room. The cinderblock walls seemed to absorb most of the light. But there was enough of it for her to see a man sitting on a cot with his head in his hands, hair slicked back. . . . and wearing a dirty white lab coat.

"Tom!" she whisper-yelled in her little girl voice, tears surfacing in her eyes. She'd found him!

CHAPTER FIFTEEN

Tom looked up at Covie, a confused twist to his eyebrows that quickly turned to a scowl. "How do you know my name?" His voice was gruff, hoarse.

She'd been so happy to see him, she forgot about her disguise. And that she had the body of an eleven-year-old beneath that disguise. "I, uh . . . I'm . . ." Where was the Covie who could spin a yarn at the drop of a hat? "Hold that thought. I'll be right back." She needed to think.

She walked down the hallway, glancing into the other cells. Charlotte's husband, Chad, and one of the other scientists were in the one next to Tom. The other two were across the hall.

Covie made her way to a small alcove. She wriggled her hand through the slit in the side of the fake raccoon skin and fumbled for her phone in her back pocket. "Stupid raccoon fingers!" she mumbled when she almost dropped it.

Staring down at the phone in her furry hand, she thought, *This isn't going to work, and I can't take this disguise off yet.* She transferred the phone into her left hand and inspected the palm side of her right. Lifting her sunglasses, she moved it closer to her face. There. A small tear in the fabric below her index finger. She pulled the rip a little wider, then snaked her finger out through the hole.

Aha! She one-finger texted Charlotte: *Found Tom.*

Charlotte texted back immediately: *That's wonderful! Is Chad okay?*

Yes. For now.

What does that mean?! Where are they?

Covie sighed. This was taking forever with one finger. *South side. By sixes casino. They want safe stuffing formula to let the guys go. Is it worth the chance? Should I talk Tom into giving to them? Or you go to police?*

Three dots flashed on the screen.

Hopefully Charlotte understood Covie's abbreviated message.

"Come on, Char," she whispered, peeking down the hallway. Still empty.

Finally, her best friend texted back: *Have Tom give them the formula. If that doesn't work, then we'll involve the police. You know they'll be reluctant to help/believe us.*

Just what she had been thinking. *Agree. TTYL.*

Be careful!!

Covie tucked her phone back inside the plush skin, into her pants pocket, and wiggled her finger back into its hiding place. With reluctance, she put the sunglasses back on. Not knowing how she would convince him—both to give up the formula and that it was her inside the raccoon—she headed back to Tom's cell with determination.

Standing as close to the bars of the cell as she could, Covie decided she had to convince him it was her first. Otherwise, he wasn't going to trust anything she told him. "Tom," she whispered, more to disguise her young voice than to keep others from hearing her. "It's me. Covie."

He stood and stepped closer to her, tilting his head to the side with a frown. "My wife is five foot ten, yet you expect me to believe she's stuffed into a child-sized . . . plush suit? Plus, your voice doesn't match Cove's." He stomped right up to the bars and grabbed the chest of the furry suit, anger sizzling in his handsome eyes. "How *did* you know my wife's name?"

"Relax, Tom! It really is me in here. I don't have time to explain, just know it's very uncomfortable in here." She couldn't tell him about being little, not yet.

He relaxed his grip, but still frowned. "Tell me something only Cove would know."

Her thoughts rushed to their daughter. "Emily was born on a Tuesday and my mom had to take me to the hospital because you were away at a conference. You barely made it in time for her birth." She paused, then softened her voice. "And you cried when you held her. You didn't even care that she was all 'gunky.'" Covie intentionally repeated the word he'd uncharacteristically used that day as he stared at his daughter for the first time.

"Cove?" His face softened for a moment until alarm took over his features. "How? How did you find me? You need to get out of here! It isn't safe. Go to the police."

Shaking her head, she said, "No. Not yet. Just listen to me, please." She didn't give him a chance to refuse, just plowed ahead. "The plush that kidnapped you all"— she spoke loud enough for all five scientists to hear her— "want the Safe Stuffing formula. That's the only way they'll let you go."

"Why? What are they going to do with it?" Tom asked.

"They want to reverse engineer it and turn all the Safe Stuffing plush into infected, animated plush so they can build up their gang and take down Plush Zero. Window and his gang want to be in charge."

"We can't do that." Tom shook his head. "That will ruin the company."

"Tom, you have to!" Covie's voice rose, sounding like a whiny little girl. She swallowed and made an effort to lower it. "They'll kill you if you don't."

He remained silent and paced in the small cell like he often did when thinking about a problem.

Covie stepped over to Charlotte's husband's cell. "Chad, please talk some sense into him. Your lives are more important than Tippy Toys."

"I'm with Covie on this one, Tom," he said. "I say we give them what they want."

"The company isn't my only concern." Tom continued to pace, arms folded at his chest. "If there was a way we could comply with their demand but neutralize the effect . . ."

Covie remained silent, letting him think. A glance at the other scientists made her realize that they knew her husband almost as well as she did. When he was figuring something out, it was best to leave him alone.

Tom stopped in front of Covie, looking at her through the bars. "I've got an idea, but it'll piss off the board of directors at Tippy Toys."

CHAPTER SIXTEEN

Tom twisted the bars like he was ringing out a wet rag. Covie leaned in.

"What if we give up the formula so they'll free us," he said, "then once we're out of this cesspool, I'll release the formula for the Safe Stuffing to the whole world. I'll just put it out there on the internet where anyone and their dog can get it."

"How would that make things better?" one of Tom's coworkers said from his own cell.

"Well, by making it public, any other plush trying to gain power will have access to make their own little faction, and that will water down the number of new members Window anticipates he'll be able to animate." Tom pinched the bridge of his nose and looked up at the ceiling for several seconds. "It will still be a disaster for Tippy Toys, but it's the best solution I can think of right now. Plus, we don't make Safe Stuffing anymore, so even though it'll be a black eye for the company, it won't totally ruin us."

"So now what?" Chad asked.

Tom touched Covie's fur-covered hand. "I'm going to

call for the ridiculous little blue guard bears. Is there a place nearby where you can hide? I don't want you to go far."

She smiled under the malodorous disguise. She was so glad she'd found him. "Yes. I'll just go back to the little alcove I hid in a few minutes ago. It's all shadowy and they won't know I'm there unless they really look."

Tom squeezed her hand/paw. "Be careful. I love you, Cove. I should be mad at you for putting yourself in danger to find me, but . . . thank you."

"I love you too. And you're welcome." Covie hurried back to the alcove and sat with her back against the wall, her knees bent, and her arms wrapped around her legs. Warmth radiated in her chest at the love she had for her husband and the relief that she'd found him alive and relatively safe. The comfort of those feelings evaporated as soon as he set the plan in motion.

"Hey! Little blue abominations! I need to talk to you!" Tom's voice carried in the cold, tunnel-like hallway.

The sound of shuffling feet came from the end of the hallway where the little bears had split off in the other direction when Covie had been following them. Quick footsteps—and deep chipmunk-like voices that reminded her of Willy Wonka's Oompa Loompas—echoed off the walls. She leaned forward to peek down toward the cells. Four of the little blue monstrosities skidded to a stop in front of Tom. "Whaddya want?" one of them asked.

"I wish to speak with Window," he said.

"Why?" the bear farthest back asked.

"Shuddup!" The bear closest to the bars of the cell elbowed the one who'd dared speak, then looked up at Tom. "Why?"

"Just tell him I'm ready to negotiate."

The supposed leader tilted its head. "Nuh-go-sh . . . what?"

Tom sighed. "Talk. Tell him I'm ready to talk."

"Why didn't you just say that, then?" the little blue bear grumbled, folding its stubby arms.

"Just go tell him before I change my mind."

"You ain't the boss of me, pris'ner."

One of the bears next to the leader nudged him and whispered something. The bears huddled in a tight circle, arguing in mumbled hisses. They broke apart and the lead bear said, "Fine. We'll go tell the boss."

Covie knew Window was nearby and wouldn't take long to send a reply, so she stayed tucked away in the alcove.

A few minutes later, the little blue bears—who seemed to have multiplied by three—led a cohort of larger plush to Tom's cell. The skunk, Stinky, stood to the side of the door with its gun drawn and nodded to a moose plush. "Okay, Horns, open the door." While the moose rattled the keys, trying to get one of them into the lock with its hooves, Stinky looked up at Tom. "You just stay nice and still-like, scientist. I'd hate to hafta shoot ya."

"Of course," Tom said.

Once the door swung open, Stinky prodded a giant black spider plush with googly eyes. "You're up, Webs. Make sure you tie him good and tight."

Wordlessly, the spider scurried into the cell and positioned itself behind Tom, holding a length of rope in its two foremost limbs.

"Hands behind ya back, human." Stinky waved the gun in Tom's direction.

He complied, and the spider wrapped the rope around his wrists, tying them together with a tight knot.

"All right," Stinky said, "let's go."

The troop of plush surrounded Tom and walked him down the hall toward the door to the bar area of the hideout. Covie slipped out of her hiding place and joined them, melding in with the group like she belonged there.

"Covie!" Chad hissed at her as she passed his cell. "What are you doing?"

She ignored him. There was no way she'd let her husband face the mobster plush on his own.

The entourage stopped in front of Window's table and Stinky nudged Tom forward with the gun.

"So," Window said, ruffling his wings. "Some of my minions tell me you want to talk." The stuffed rooster tipped its head to look at him with its unpatched eye. "So talk."

Tom stood straight, peering down at the mob boss. "I heard that there's something you want from my colleagues and me. Something that we may be willing to give you in exchange for our release."

"Oh? And what did you hear that I want?"

"Rumors being what they are and all, it would make more sense for you to tell me—just in case I heard wrong." Tom's voice held an edge Covie hadn't heard before.

Window stared at him, tapping his three toes on the table. When Tom didn't continue after an uncomfortable fifteen seconds, the rooster plush cleared its throat. "Fine. I want the Safe Stuffing formula."

Tom nodded. "And if I give it to you?"

"Then I'll set you all free, of course." Window's beak curved up into a lopsided smile.

"Okay. It's a deal." Tom looked over his shoulder at his bound hands. "I'll need a pen and paper, and you'll need to free my hands so I can write it down."

When Tom finished writing the complicated formula

from memory, he laid the pen down and pushed the notebook toward Window.

The plush mob boss lifted its beak and crowed. He turned to the skunk plush. "Stinky, shoot them. All five of them."

CHAPTER SEVENTEEN

"No!" Covie pushed her way to the table. She lowered her voice and tried to gain control of her emotions. "Uhh . . . boss, that's, umm, cool, if that's what you want to do." She shrugged to show Window just how okay with shooting the scientists she was. "But, uhh, what if we need to employ this tactic again? No kidnappee is going to want to cooperate with you if you go back on your word, right?"

Window nodded slowly, looking raccoon Covie up and down. "Yeah. Pretty smart for a waitress." He swept a wing around at the plush crowded about his table. "Why didn't one of you numbskulls think of that?"

"I was just about to say the exact same thing, boss," the moose with the keys said. "The raccoon just beat me to it."

Window shook his head. "Whatever, Horns." He put the tip of his wing up to the side of his face and narrowed his eye. "Okay, so no killing them. But I am going to change the deal."

Tom's head snapped up, his lips pulled tight over his teeth, to stare at the rooster.

"Yeah," Window said. "Here's the new deal: We'll

keep the scientists so *they* can reverse engineer the formula. I mean, why would I spend my efforts working on it when I have a group of scientists at my fingertips?" He looked down at the skunk. "Take him back to his cell."

The spider plush scurried over and bound Tom's hands again before the large group of plush escorted him back to the small room. Covie stayed with them and followed some of them down the other hallway when they dispersed. Only one of the little blue bears remained, a ring of keys hanging from its arm.

She watched from the doorway of a darkened supply room. The little guard walked past her as it made its rounds, and unlocked then exited through a door at the end of the hall. A brief triangle of sunlight engulfed the blue bear before the door closed behind it.

Making sure she was alone, Covie returned to Tom's cell. She sat on the floor close to the bars, while her husband sat on a stool on the other side.

"You saved me back there. Not just me, but all of us." Tom gestured to the cells holding his fellow scientists. "Thank you."

"You're welcome. Again." She added a teasing lilt to her voice since he couldn't see her smile. "But now I need to figure out a way to get you all out of here. That chicken is not stable, and I don't trust him as far as he can fly."

Tom took on the professorial tone he always used when science-splaining something to her—or Emily, or a waiter, or some random stranger on the street. "Window is actually a rooster—well, the plush version of a rooster. And roosters don't really fly, their bodies are too big for their little wings to get enough lift—"

"I know, Tom." Covie laughed. Sometimes his habit of "teaching" her and everyone else was annoying, but mostly she found it endearing, just part of who he was. "I just meant that I don't trust him at all."

"Oh. Yes. Right." He cleared his throat. "But back to escaping—I think you should just get yourself out of here while you can, Cove. You get out and then call the police. At least that way Emily will still have one of us if . . . something happens."

She shook her head. "I'm not leaving you here, so just forget about that." Her head pounded and she rubbed at her temples through the disguise. "I need to figure this out fast. I can't stay inside this stinking plush skin much longer."

"You do have quite a nauseating odor about you."

"You should smell it from the inside."

"Are you going to tell me how you squeezed yourself in there now?" Tom asked.

Panic constricted her throat. He would think she was crazy if she tried to tell him she'd woken up as a younger version of herself. And now was not the time to try to explain anyway; the priority was to get Tom and the others out of here alive.

The echo of rattling keys bounced off the cinderblock walls from the other hallway. Covie stood and hurried to the alcove, a plan forming in her mind. She pulled the machete out and held her breath, waiting.

The guard walked past the barred cells, mocking the scientists. "Can't believe you thought you'd get outta here that easy." It cackled. "The boss ain't stupid. He wasn't born yesterday."

He wasn't born *at all, you imbecile,* Covie thought. The shuffling feet and rattling keys neared her hiding place. She gripped the machete tighter and pounced when the guard appeared in front of her. With one swipe, she took its head off, kicking it down the hall like a soccer ball, blood and stuffing gore leaving a streak on the dirty tile.

She grabbed the keys and sprinted to the first cell, struggling a little to fit the key in the lock with plush raccoon hands gloved over her own.

"What now?" one of the scientists asked as he stepped out of the cramped cell.

"Let me get the others out and then I'll take you to the exit." Covie was already turning the lock on the next cell.

She reached Tom's cell last, wanting to throw her arms around him as soon as she flung the door open. But they needed to hurry, and her neat-freak husband would not appreciate the nasty alcoholic plush skin wrapping around him anyway. "Follow me."

Running as fast as her short legs would allow, Covie rounded the corner to the other hallway, skidding on the no-traction raccoon feet before continuing to the exit door she'd seen the guard use.

They reached the door and she fumbled with the keys, finally fitting the right one in the padlock barring their exit. The door to the casino and bar crashed into the wall at the other end as a gang of plush barreled through.

"There they are! Get them!"

Covie flung the door open and held it as she ushered Tom and his fellow scientists through, keeping her eyes on the approaching plush.

"Come on, Cove!" Tom yelled.

"Just go!" She pushed him outside. "I'll find another way out!" She slammed the door, clamped the padlock shut, and broke the key off in the lock.

CHAPTER EIGHTEEN

Covie dashed to a stairwell on her right. The stairs going to the upper floors were blocked with a metal gate, so she headed down, holding tight to her machete. The stairs led to an eerie subterranean vault that stretched on for what seemed like miles, branching off into tunnels at unpredictable intervals. Pipes of all sizes spanned the ceiling and walls, and strange noises pinged around inside them.

The plush posse spilled down the stairs after her, making a racket with their yells and various weaponized objects. Covie chanced a glance behind her, shocked to see a trio of the tiny blue bears closing in on her. How were they so fast on their short little legs? She skewered them one at a time on the tip of her machete, then turned down one of the tunnels as they wriggled like worms on a hook, cursing her as she held them aloft like a banner.

As she ran, she swiped the bears off on a pipe running along the wall, her big knife now covered in their sticky gore. She turned left down yet another tunnel, dimly lit with yellowing bulbs that flickered dizzyingly.

Covie jerked forward as something slammed into her back.

"Bull's-eye!"

The triumphant shout came from right behind her. She whirled around to face the oncoming horde, dancing to keep from tripping over the baseball wrapped in barbed wire that had been thrown at her. A purple sloth stretched out, aiming a sawed-off shotgun at her. With a snarl, Covie lopped off both of its arms and kicked them and the gun under a pipe.

The injured sloth sprayed blood all over its cohorts and was soon trampled beneath the hooves, feet, and paws of those around it, rushing toward Covie.

Her raging adrenaline allowed her to focus on the plush with guns, ignoring those with less lethal weapons. She chopped off Stinky's head, but its body stayed standing and its hands fired a shot that ricocheted off the cement floor in front of her. Stinky's head rolled, chomping at anything in its path. So she stomped down on the headless skunk and pushed the gun under the pipe with her foot.

Something tugged at her leg. She swung the machete in a wide swath to clear some space before looking down. A green dragon with a corkscrew attached to its tail with a zip tie had punctured the leg of the plush skin she wore and was now tugging it back and forth to try to dislodge it. Covie stepped on the dragon's head with her other foot and yanked her nearly impaled leg back with a jerk. Both the head and tail of the plush separated from its body with a rip, the tail still hanging from her leg.

The dwindling number of plush parted slightly and a remote-controlled monster truck barreled toward her, two sharp pieces of jagged metal duct-taped to the roll bar. Whoever controlled it was skilled. The truck dashed in and ripped a piece of her disguise at her knee, then reversed out of her reach before she could smash it. A drone flew in from the side and slammed into her, but got caught in the gash it had created in the raccoon head. Covie grasped it with her left hand and threw it against the wall with a crash.

The monster truck had retreated out of her sight. She stomped and slashed the machete at the plush gang, decreasing their numbers even further. The truck sped toward her again, loaded down with at least five of the little blue bears. It crashed into her shins and the bears leaped onto her, slashing into the raccoon skin with tooth-brushes, sharpened on the end like some sort of shiv from a plush prison. Covie ripped three of them off the front of her and tore their heads off before flinging them down the hall. The other two had climbed to her back. She turned and jumped backward against the wall, smashing the bears into the cement.

The RC truck retreated again, and she watched it as she slashed at anything that came near her. Two dol-phins hid between pipes, holding remotes. Covie rushed them, driving the tip of her machete into one's forehead while the other one flopped itself under a pipe where she couldn't reach it. She jumped on the monster truck with both feet, smashing it so the tires splayed to either side.

"Window!" one of the few remaining plush yelled.

Covie looked up in time to brace herself as the rooster, riding the moose plush, slammed into her. She fell to her butt and stabbed upward as the moose tumbled over her, slicing it from chest to flank. Blood and cotton gore cov-ered her, and she scrambled back, her feet slipping on the wet surface, as Window charged her with the sharp edge of a broken wine bottle thrust toward her.

She knocked the bottle from its wings as she rolled to the side and got to her knees. She speared the machete through his chest and into the pipe behind him. Her hand, now covered in plush blood, slipped from the handle when she tried to pull it out.

Window gaped at her as he hung suspended from the knife through his chest.

CHAPTER NINETEEN

The few remaining plush ran back the way they'd come.

Window's eye patch had slipped off, revealing a gaping hole where a polished plastic eye used to be. He stared at Covie with his remaining eye and coughed, blood trickling out the side of his beak. "You're a little girl?"

Covie looked down at her disguise, now in tatters, exposing her true form.

"Little girls . . . are supposed to love plush."

"Yeah? Well plush are supposed to be loveable."

Window smiled, parting his felt beak.

"Where's Plush Zero?!" Covie yelled.

"Why would a little girl want something so vile as Plush Zero? You know he's not going to snuggle with you. In fact, he's going to kill all of you!" Window coughed, light-pink froth forming around his beak. "He's too powerful."

"Where is he? I need to know."

Window stared blankly into her eyes.

Did a fiber of guilt course through her? Was she feeling bad for the evil rooster?

The plush slumped and looked past her into oblivion.

Covie shook her head and reminded herself that these

plush and this plushdemic were the embodiment of some unknown microbe infection. Her guilt subsided. She stood shoulders back, then used her foot for leverage and pulled the machete free, dropping the mob boss to the ground. She swung the blade, decapitating Window, then pulled all the stuffing out of the rooster's body and head, leaving a lifeless husk.

Making her way back to the stairs, Covie beheaded any of the plush she found injured but still moving, knowing they only needed to reunite their heads with their bodies in order to continue on. But that was all she had time for. Removing their stuffing would take too long and she needed to get out of there before word spread and the rest of the gang returned to the roost.

As she reached the stairs, her arms fell to her sides and she almost lost her grip on the machete. Exhaustion like she'd never known invaded her body. "Guess I used up all my adrenaline," she murmured. The stairs seemed insurmountable. The temptation to just sit and rest for a few minutes grew strong. She deserved to rest, right? She hadn't really slept since the night of the body swap.

Covie sighed.

She would rest later. It was too dangerous here and now. She switched hands with her machete, not daring to put it away just yet. She looked down, remembering that her disguise was nothing but a ragged mess hanging off her body. No longer much of a disguise. She set the knife down and peeled the remains of the raccoon plush off. Her sunglasses had been lost somewhere during the fight. *Dang it!* They'd been expensive. A jolt of alarm hit her and she reached for her back pocket, relieved to find her phone was still with her.

She put the machete back in its sheath still taped to

her leg—she'd be able to get to it easily now if she needed it—and trudged up the stairs.

Reaching the door to Window's hideout, she put her ear against it and listened. Hearing nothing, she opened it, one hand on the handle of her machete. Not a soul remained in the bar. Half-drunk drinks and half-eaten meals sat among scattered cards, dice, and cash. Covie helped herself to an untouched hamburger, chasing it down with a warm whiskey neat. On the table where Window and his crew had been sitting lay the notebook Tom had written the formula in. She grabbed it and thumbed through it. "Yes!" She stared down at a list of claw machine locations that Window and his crew had collected. She stuffed the notebook in her tattered, not-so-sparkly-now backpack and exited into the alley.

She scanned the area and whisper-yelled, "Tom!" Nothing, no movement. *Good, they listened. Safe for now.*

Covie made her way back to her car just as the streetlamps came on—the ones that weren't broken, anyway. She put the machete back in the outside pocket of the backpack and slung it onto the passenger seat before slumping into the driver's seat. She hit the door lock button and rested her head against the steering wheel. Knowing she couldn't stay in this neighborhood where the plush reigned, she forced herself to sit up and start the car. She drove to a parking garage with twenty-four-hour security and swiped her credit card for entrance.

The lighting was dim, but dim was better than none. She parked away from other cars, checking again that the doors were locked. She quickly shot off a text to Char, thankful her fingers were no longer obstructed in the raccoon carcass.

Covie: *Hey I got them out!*

Char: *Thank you, thank you so much! I'm so relieved!!!!*

Covie: *Me too.*

Char: *Did you tell Tom about you being a little girl?*

Covie: *Not yet.*

Char: *Okay.*

Covie: *I will now.*

Char: *Sounds good.*

* * *

Covie: *Tom, I need to talk to you.*

Tom: *Where are you?*

Covie: *I'm safe, but I need your help.*

Tom: *I'll come to you.*

Covie: *I went back to the hospital.*

Tom: *What?! I just saw you in the racoon plush?*

Covie didn't know why she wanted to keep up the ruse.

Covie: *The Phyzcoxin is acting up again. SynthNA is monitoring me and I have to quarantine.*

She hated herself for being compelled to keep up this falsehood. But then she quickly justified it.

Phyzcoxin had been in trial phase. Tom had been

against Covie taking it at the beginning. It had been too new. He had needed to do research on it first. It had been too experimental, but Covie had pushed and pushed. She had called it instinct. There wasn't any alternative at the time so she had met with SynthNA and decided to let them administer the treatments without Tom knowing. The night before she had treatment, she broke it to him that she was going to do it. She hadn't wanted to go behind his back, but his scientist brain hadn't formed any conclusions, and it had taken too long for him to come around. Eventually, though, he had got on board with it.

> **Tom:** *I'm so sorry you have to quarantine again. I knew I should have looked into it more.*

> **Covie:** *Tom, don't do that. It's not that. Everything will be all right.*

> **Tom:** *Okay.*

> **Covie:** *Trust me.*

> **Tom:** *Okay.*

> **Covie:** *I love you.*

> **Tom:** *Love you too.*

Covie held her phone to her chest. A swath of light from the screen lit up the brown spots of dried blood all over her neck. She sniffed, and then tears cascaded down her dirty cheeks. As she cried in the dark car, she started to feel guilty. She needed Tom.

Covie convinced herself that Tom could help her, but she'd just lied to him.

> **Covie:** *Tom, are you still awake?*

Tom: *Yes*

Covie: *I lied to you.*

Tom: *What do you mean?*

Covie: *I'm going to come over to the house tomorrow and we can talk. I have to show you something and I need your help.*

Tom: *Ummm, Okay. Is it about the formula?*

Covie: *I don't have to quarantine, but something is wrong.*

No text.

Covie: *Tom?*

No text.

Covie: *Are you still there?*

No text.

Covie's heart started to thump inside her flat chest. She scooted down in the seat and slumped, letting her head kink onto the seat belt. With the phone in her lap, her eyes closed, squishing out a flood of tears.

Just as she was drifting into an exhausted state of sleep, her phone buzzed. She flipped it over and looked. A text from Tom sat in the banner.

Tom: *I'm so sorry, Char came over.*

Covie: *Oh Okay.*

Char was just doing what Covie had asked her to do—watch over her family.

Covie: *Did she tell you what's wrong with me?*

No text.

Covie: *Tom?*

No text.

Tom: *Sorry, we are making some dinner.*

Covie: *Is Chad there?*

Tom: *Not yet, but he's coming. Char wanted to celebrate. Come home, and we can all be together. Tomorrow, we can get this all figured out. I don't care that you lied, whatever that means. If you don't have to quarantine, then come home. We can figure all this out in the morning.*

Covie looked down at herself. She was filthy. Completely unpresentable. Since nothing had changed with her predicament, she was compelled to just text him until she could get cleaned up. She wanted to let them celebrate. She wanted Tom and Emily to have a good night without the incredible shrinking woman to freak everyone out.

Covie: *I'll come by tomorrow and we can talk. Is that okay?*

Tom: *I can come to you.*

Covie: *It's okay. I'm safe. I'll come tomorrow.*

Tom: *Sure, Cove. I love you.*

She crawled into the back seat, clutched her phone to her chest like a pre-plushdemic kitty plush, and slept.

Covie sat up, every muscle in her body stiff and sore like she'd run a marathon. She looked down at her hands, disappointed to see that they hadn't transformed back into grown-up hands. She grimaced at the dried plush blood and strands of stuffing stuck to her skin and clothes. A real shower was her top priority, but where? A young child covered in blood and gore would only bring questions and trouble. It was early—maybe she could find an empty model home or something. But no, she was sure they'd all be equipped with alarms.

She leaned her head back against the seat. She was grateful that her courage to go tell Tom hadn't dissipated through the night. Covie couldn't wait to go home, but she couldn't let her mom or Emily or Tom see her like this. Her thoughts returned to getting cleaned up.

Something about showers tickled her memory. Where had she seen public showers? She sat up, her muscles screaming at the abrupt move. The lake! It was about a fifteen-minute drive, and there were outdoor showers on the boardwalk by the beach—and it should be deserted there at this early hour. She plugged her phone in to charge and headed there.

After stripping down to her tank top and underwear, Covie scrubbed herself under the cold water, heart racing as she watched for visitors. She kept her backpack and machete within lunging distance in case any pervo pedophiles showed up.

When she figured she was clean enough, she grabbed her backpack and hurried to the public bathroom to change into her last set of clean clothes—pink sweatpants with a sparkling heart on the thigh and a T-shirt with "Love" written in sequins across the front. She didn't have any clean socks, so she forced her naked, damp feet into her daughter's boots. The soiled clothes were stuffed into a nearby trash can, then she clomped back to her car to have a protein bar breakfast.

The notebook she'd taken from Window's hideout lay on top of the food. Covie set it on her lap and flipped through it as she ate. Coming to the page with the Safe Stuffing formula, she ran her fingers over her husband's precise handwriting—even in a moment of duress, it was better than hers.

"Should I still release this to the public?" she wondered out loud.

CHAPTER TWENTY

With Window dead, what would happen to his plan? Covie was pretty sure she knew: His gang's survivors would carry it out. The raven, the snake, the pig—none of them had participated in the battle yesterday. Which meant they'd all escaped. And they all knew about the plan.

She looked down at the notebook in her lap. They didn't have the formula, though. Shaking her head, Covie thought, *I don't know that for sure. They could have taken a picture of it or something. There was a lot of time between Tom writing it down and the escape.*

Releasing the formula would deter Window's gang from carrying out his plan to create an army out of the Safe Stuffing plush from the claw machines. And guarantee Tom and the other scientists wouldn't be kidnapped again for the formula. Letting anyone access it would water down all the factions. Any little plush with an ounce of hubris could challenge Plush Zero, and now Window's gang. It should deter any group of plush from kidnapping the scientists again. That decided it for her.

Starting with social media, she published the formula

with a brief explanation. Then she sent it to all the news outlets she could think of. She felt a twinge of guilt that doing so would likely ruin Tippy Toys, but Tom and the other scientists were safe, and that's what mattered most. Plus, how bad could it be? Tippy Toys hadn't produced Safe Stuffing in a long time.

* * *

Covie *had* to see her family. Just a peek to make sure Tom and Emily were okay. She parked down the block after the sun had set and walked to her house. A flood of emotions hit her in the chest when her house came into view. It had only been a couple of days, but it felt like much longer, and worse, she had no idea when—or even if— this nightmare would be over.

She wiped the tears from her face and snuck across the lawn to hide in the bushes in front of the living room window. Emily skipped into the room, laughing and smiling. Tom and Charlotte entered right behind her, and he lifted the remote from the arm of his chair and turned the TV on. They stood and watched as "Breaking News" flashed across the large screen. The volume was up loud enough that Covie could hear it through the open window.

A picture of Tippy Toys headquarters was displayed in the corner of the screen as a young reporter spoke. "Tippy Toys' Safe Stuffing formula was released to the public this morning by an anonymous individual with a cryptic message that said, 'To protect the scientists. No more kidnappings.' Tippy Toys' stock dropped precipitously after the leaked formula made it to the national news media, even though the company had discontinued the program years ago."

The reporter turned to a different monitor and continued, "A spokesperson from the toy company responsible for making plush safe again said they have opened an internal investigation into the leak and have no other comments at this time.

"Calls have ramped up for Tippy Toys to destroy all Safe Stuffing plush and demolish existing claw machines. Citizens of Dia Metro City have already taken this into their own hands. Over to you, Sandra."

The video feed switched to Sandra standing in front of a burning pile of Safe Stuffing plush and a group of claw machines. A gray-bearded man stood next to the reporter.

"What is going on here?" the reporter asked.

"This is the first drop zone where people can drop Safe Stuffing plush off and we will destroy it without any cost. If Tippy Toys won't take care of Safe Stuffing plush, we will. We never asked for more plush in our world. They shoved these plush onto us—"

The reporter and gray-bearded man were interrupted when a group of people started beating the claw machines with baseball bats and sledge hammers. Sandra jumped at the sound of breaking plexiglass and denting metal.

"Back to you in the studio, Ryan," she eventually said.

"Thank you, Sandra. This has been a breaking news story. Tune in to *News at Nine* for updates. We now return you to your previously scheduled program."

Tom shook his head and said something to Charlotte.

Was this the wrong move? Covie thought. *I saved them. And this was the right thing to do.* She justified releasing the formula and possibly ruining not only hers and Tom's lives but Charlotte's and Chad's, and the other scientists and their spouses.

Covie smiled. She hadn't mentioned this to Tom and

the other scientists, but that had been part of her plan. She wanted to draw Plush Zero out of his hiding place for two reasons: to get him to tell her how to reverse the effects of what the booby-trapped claw machine had done to her, and to capture him so Biotoy could use him to create a cure for the plushdemic.

The claw machines full of Safe Stuffing plush were the perfect bait. Now she was home and she could let Tom in on her plan. Covie walked up the front walk, but before she could get to the door, Emily turned toward the window and smiled at her, waving with one hand while holding a walrus plush in the other. Charlotte, noticing Emily waving, turned and looked directly at Covie. With a slight nod of her head, she put an arm around Covie's daughter, pulled her against her side, and guided her to turn back toward the TV. Charlotte touched Tom's arm and laughed at something on the show now playing.

A pang of jealousy caused Covie to narrow her eyes at her best friend. But she shook it off. Char was just doing what she'd asked her to do—looking after her family while she was unable to be there.

Covie was home now. Tom could start helping her heal and figure this all out. They could do this together. She felt strange knocking, but it seemed appropriate in her current condition. The last thing she wanted to do was to start with everyone questioning why a little girl barged into the house.

Emily came to the door and pulled it open. Covie was glad her daughter was so friendly to girls her age.

"Hi," Covie said.

Emily smiled. "Hi." She hugged the walrus.

"Who is it?" Tom asked.

"Who *are* you?" Emily asked.

Covie didn't answer. "Is your dad here?"

"Dad!" Emily yelled over her shoulder toward the front room.

Tom and Char approached the open front door.

Char put her hands on Emily's shoulders. "Em, why don't you go to your room for a bit?"

That was weird, Covie thought.

"Hello, little girl," Char started.

Covie tilted her head and widened her eyes.

"How can we help you?" Tom asked.

Covie could feel her pulse thump in her ears. "Um." She looked at Tom and resisted the urge to lunge and hug him. "Tom, it's Cove," she said, stepping forward.

Char took a step back and pulled Tom with her. "Stay right there, little girl."

"Char," Covie started, "you know me. We talked right here the other day."

"Tom"—Char turned to her husband—"I think she's with them. I think this little girl works with the plush," she blurted out.

Tom took a step back under his own volition.

Covie fought back tears. This was all unraveling. It was not the reunion she had imagined last night when she was falling asleep. She needed Tom's help. She wanted her best friend to support her.

"But it really is me," she said. "There was an accident, Tom. I think the claw machine did something to me."

"How did you know about that?!" he demanded.

"Because I'm Covie!"

"Oh, they're good." Char talked directly to Tom. "Can't you see? They did the research. They know Cove touched a claw machine. She's either kidnapped and they tortured her to get this info, or she's probably working with them! Let's call the police."

Not listening to Charlotte, Tom stepped forward. "What did you do to my wife?"

"I didn't do anything to her! I am your wife!" Covie yelled.

"Come on, Tom." Char stood between them. "Let's try to salvage what's left of today. I'll get dinner going."

Charlotte started to close the door.

"Tom! Please let me talk to you!" She couldn't hold it any longer. Tears gushed from her eyes. She wiped her cheeks on the back of her arm, and between snuffling, she said, "It really is me. I got shrunk somehow."

Tom's mouth was agape. He didn't say anything. Covie knew, though. His scientist mind was trying to make sense of this. But before he could conclude what he was witnessing, her best friend closed the door.

Covie's shoulders fell and she walked back to the car slouched. Why didn't Charlotte recognize her? Maybe she should go back and try again. What was she going to do now? The only thing she knew was that she needed to find Plush Zero and the claw machine with the narwal and unicorn sticker now!

Covie drove around aimlessly until she realized it was getting late. She wanted to go to the public library to do some research before it closed. She never thought she'd regret not listening to Tom's constant prattle about the plush pandemic and plush and stuffing and blah, blah, blah. But now she did.

"We close in thirty minutes," the lady at the desk said as Covie walked in.

"Okay, I just need to use a computer for a few minutes."

"Do you have a library card?" she asked.

Crap. "Umm . . . I forgot to bring it. Can you look it up?"

The librarian sighed. "Sure. What's your name and address?"

Covie gave her Emily's name.

"Okay. It looks like your dad gave you permission to use the computers, but that permission expired a month ago." Her face softened as she looked at Covie. "But I'll let you use it this one time. Just make sure you get the permission slip signed again for next time." She handed Covie the slip.

Covie nodded, then found the most secluded computer in the library and sat in front of it. Starting with government documents that had been released to the public, she read about the bombing of 2033. It had been a failure, of course. The Army's attempts at killing off the infected plush had resulted in extreme damage to the areas bombed and hadn't even come close to killing them off. In addition, the plushdemic proliferated at every bomb site. It was like the bombs created a chain reaction—a mitosis of sorts.

Her phone buzzed in her pocket; before looking she knew it was Tom. There was no way she could answer it— her little voice would never convince him now. Instead, she shot him a text.

> **Covie:** *Hey, I have terrible service, what's up?*
>
> **Tom:** *Are you okay? Some little girl just stopped by claiming to be you. Where are you?*

She paused for a moment, wishing she could make him believe it truly had been her.

With that, she shoved her phone into her pocket and didn't look to see if Tom replied.

With that out of the way, she could go back to tracking down more information on Plush Zero—she didn't even know what kind of plush it was. She turned to news stories, eyewitness accounts, blog posts, and social media posts. All she found was a lot of speculation and the occasional crazy person or conspiracy theory podcasts that claimed to know Plush Zero. Trouble was, they all claimed it was a different plush.

CHAPTER
TWENTY-ONE

"Library closes in ten minutes," the librarian announced to Covie and the only other patron in the place, a college-aged man using the printer.

Covie cleared the search history on the computer and turned it off. She got to her feet slowly, not looking forward to another night in her car. Exiting through the back, she made a last-minute decision and put a small rock in the doorway to prop it open. She watched from the park across the street, rubbing her arms as the evening chill set in. The librarian exited through the front, a big ring of keys dangling as she locked the tall old doors. Her thick heels clacked as she walked hurriedly to her car, then drove away.

Crossing her fingers that the librarian hadn't noticed the propped door, Covie made her way to the back of the building. The door opened easily, and she did a fist pump with a quiet "Yes!"

Covie knew exactly where she would spend the night in the large library. She headed for the children's section, to a small wood cabin that would make a cozy little sleeping spot. As she reached for the child-sized door, her hand shook. She really needed to eat. Now that she'd noticed the gnawing hunger, it was all she could think about.

She made her way to the coffee shop and climbed over the half-door, surprised and pleased that the glass-covered pastry shelves weren't locked. A little bit of guilt crept into her shrinking stomach as she procured a cheese Danish, a small lemon pound cake, and a bottle of water from the shop. *This is paid for with my tax dollars, so really, I own a stake in this business,* she thought. But it wasn't enough to assuage her guilt. "Fine," she said out loud to the cash register, its red light blinking at her accusingly, "I'll make a good-sized donation to the library when this is all over."

Inside the little cabin, Covie ate the spoils of her thievery, then snuggled in to sleep—a squishy Safe Stuffing plush puppy as a pillow and an elephant as her mattress. She pinched the cloth label in the outside leg of the elephant.

Tippy Toys, Inc. This plush was made with love and Safe Stuffing.

The smell and feel of the plush reminded her too much of Window and his gang, so in a moment of total freak-out, she threw the plush out into the reading circle with the child-sized chairs and tables.

Her final thought as she drifted off to sleep was of the last encounter she had with Charlotte, Tom, and Emily.

* * *

Covie awoke to the sound of a vacuum and an off-key voice singing above the droning of the machine.

Crap. She hadn't thought about a cleaning crew coming in early. She rubbed her eyes and ran her fingers through her tangled hair. The vacuum seemed to be moving away from her, so now was a good time to make her escape. She peeked out the window of her little sanctuary. The coast was clear. As she made her way past a row of bookshelves toward the back exit, she spied the housekeeper, a short man with a balding head, earphones covering his ears, dancing some sort of cha-cha while he pushed the vacuum, his back facing her. She slunk out the door and released a heavy breath as it closed behind her.

Back in her car, she pulled Window's notebook out and turned to the pages where the claw machine locations were listed. She ran her finger down the list and stopped at an abandoned toy store in the city. It had once been the biggest in the whole state—it even had a gigantic Ferris wheel at the three-story entrance. But the advent of online shopping followed by the plush pandemic had been hard on brick-and-mortar toy stores. Emily's favorite place to go when they went to the city had closed down about six months ago. That's where Covie would start, where there wouldn't be anyone around to bother her.

Entering the deserted store was as easy as prying some plywood off a window in the back where the loading dock was. Having a smaller body came in handy for such breaking-and-entering endeavors—though Covie wouldn't even be there if it weren't for that same small body.

The emergency lights remained on, casting a dim glow to see by. She found the claw machine among empty shelves and scattered garbage. It didn't have the scratched purple narwhal or unicorn stickers. Her spirit fell a little and she frowned—it wasn't *her* claw machine, the one from the Stop a Sec. She reached in her pocket for the loose change she'd dug out of the console of her car and fed it into the machine anyway. She was there, she might as well give it a try. Maybe this machine was boo-by-trapped too, and could change her back.

The claw closed over a small plush snake, a smaller version of Window's goon with the lisp, and it dropped into the prize drawer. Covie inhaled a big breath and held it as she reached in to retrieve the plush. Her hand closed over it and . . . nothing. No shock or burn. No alteration of her child's body.

Dropping the snake to the floor, she tried again. An adorable yellow duckling with a wide orange beak dangled from the claw, barely making it to the edge of the prize drawer before slipping out of its grasp. This time Covie didn't hesitate to grab it. Again . . . nothing.

Several minutes later, out of change and with a pile of useless plush at her feet, Covie's frustration boiled over. She kicked the claw machine, doing nothing more than hurting her toe and further scuffing her daughter's boot. With a childish growl, she picked up the plush and threw them down a nearby toy aisle.

She stared at her distorted reflection in the plexiglass of the claw machine and an idea hatched in her mind.

CHAPTER
TWENTY-TWO

A large empty box tipped on its side provided the perfect hiding place for Covie. She positioned it down a garbage-strewn aisle, in the dark shadows of the looming shelves, where she could keep her eye on the claw machine but couldn't easily be seen herself. She slipped her arms out of the backpack straps and scooted into the box, crossing her legs like circle time in kindergarten. She pulled the backpack in next to her, the machete handle within easy reach, as she watched and waited, hoping that releasing the Safe Stuffing formula would spur Plush Zero on, causing him to come for the plush in the claw machines.

The box soon became warm with Covie's body heat, and her head bobbed as she tried to keep herself awake. The boredom was relentless. How did the police deal with this when they were on stakeouts? Doughnuts? She rested her head against the side of the box and gave in to the pull of her heavy eyelids.

"Hey, guys! I found it!" a scruffy voice called.

Covie jerked awake, shaking the box she hid in. She blinked until the claw machine came into focus. A scraggly tiger plush missing most of the fur on its shoulder stood with its nose pressed up against the plexiglass. Four more ragged plush joined it. Her heart pounded in her rib cage. This was it!

Could this be Plush Zero and his gang? If so, they weren't what Covie had pictured.

"How're we gonna get them out?" a soiled spotted fawn asked.

"Just break the glass." The orangutan demonstrated by slamming the broken hockey stick it had in place of its right arm against the plexiglass. It bounced off and hit the plush in the face.

"That ain't no real glass," the plush said. It was now missing its nose, which had fallen off when the hockey stick ricocheted back on it.

All five plush pounded on the glass with various hard objects. After several minutes, the tiger dropped the rock it had been using and leaned up against the machine. "This ain't working."

"Let's try tipping it over," the fawn suggested.

Covie had to stifle a laugh as the small- to medium-sized plush pushed on the reinforced claw machine. It didn't so much as shift a millimeter.

A tall shadow materialized above the bumbling group. Covie covered her mouth as the shadow's owner stepped into view. The man's duster, made of long strips of free-hanging plush pelts, flowed about him as he made short work of slaughtering the five plush trying to break into the claw machine. The large kitchen knife sliced through their plush necks like they were made of melted butter, the dim light glinting off its razor-sharp edge.

The man pulled the stuffing out of the beheaded plush, working with the precision of a practiced surgeon—or serial killer. Over and over he worked as headless bodies crawled toward him.

"Why, sir?" the fawn pleaded. "Why'd you do it?"

No answer came as the man shoved his hand into the bodiless head, ripping red stuffing from within.

Covie watched from her hiding place, fascinated by the metal plague-doctor mask he wore. Three or four pieces of irregular-sized metal were patched together with bad welds and bolts. His left eye was exposed down to the cheekbone, where the metal had been cut to reveal a striking blue eye. A thick green lens covered the right eye. And that wasn't even the weirdest thing about the mask. Covie's forehead creased as she tried to figure out what the two corrugated tubes flowing from the tip of the mask's beak were for. One tube was a smaller diameter than the other, and they both wrapped over his head and plugged into the left temple area of the mask.

Once finished with the gutting of the animated plush, he slid his knife into a utility belt beneath his duster and pulled out a small black case from a different pocket of the belt. The strangely clad man knelt at the back of the claw machine and unzipped the case, revealing a collection of neatly arranged tools as he set it on the ground. Using what looked to Covie like a small screwdriver, he meticulously opened the lower half of the machine, removing the small screws from the metal covering with quick twists of the tool.

When he had the circuit board exposed, he let it hang by the wires attaching it to the machine while he put the little screwdriver back in the case and removed another tool resembling needle-nosed pliers. He disconnected some of the wires from the board, and the plexiglass door popped open with a click. Covie was impressed—he'd just picked the electronic lock as smoothly as she could pick a key lock.

One by one, the man pulled the plush out of the machine, cut the heads off, and pulled the clean light-blue stuffing out.

Safe Stuffing, Covie thought.

She worked up the courage to leave her hiding place—they were on the same team, after all, weren't they? She scooted out of the box, dragging the backpack with her, and stood, pulling her machete out. She picked up the few plush she'd thrown down the aisle earlier and handed them to him as he stared at her with his piercing blue eye. Without a word, he sliced off the head of the snake and removed the stuffing. Covie picked up the duck and did the same, knowing their actions would prevent these plush from becoming animated once the Safe Stuffing formula had been reversed.

When every plush within sight had been decapitated and gutted, Covie wiped the stuffing fibers off her machete with one of the many papers littering the floor, then slipped it into its sheath in the backpack. The man followed her movements with his blue eye. With a satisfied nod, he picked up the fresh plush pelts and packed them into a sack he then slung over his shoulder like some alternate version of Jim Bridger Santa Claus.

She carefully stood, taking in the scene. Small piles of oozing red clumps of plushdemic stuffing littered the tile floor. Light-blue Safe Stuffing soaked up puddles of plush blood.

The man fixed his uncovered eye on Covie. "What are you doing here?"

She shrugged, not sure she could trust this stranger. "You first. What's your name and why are *you* here?"

The skin around his exposed eye crinkled like he'd smiled beneath the mask. "I'm Mac Raiden. Your turn."

Was that his real name? She had no way of knowing. She took a step forward and slipped on the crimson gore.

Regaining her balance, she held out her hand. "I'm Covie."

CHAPTER
TWENTY-THREE

Covie put her hands on her hips and looked Mac in the eye. "How about you answer my other question. Why are you here?"

He let out a huff that was maybe a laugh. "I asked first, little girl."

Her eyebrows made a V on her forehead. "I am not—" She folded her arms and glared at him while she thought. He *did* ask first. But Covie wasn't convinced she could trust him to know everything about her yet. "Fine. I want to help find a cure for the plush pandemic, and I heard that Plush Zero is the key to that. I thought he or his cronies might be interested in these claw machines now that the Safe Stuffing formula has been released. So I decided to start here."

Nodding, Mac adjusted the sack full of plush pelts on his shoulder. "Smart girl."

His evasion of her question was starting to annoy her. "Now you. What are you doing here?"

The piercing blue eye stared at her through the open spot in his mask. Refusing to be intimidated by the stranger, Covie stared right back.

After several seconds of the standoff, Mac shrugged.

"Same as you. Mostly. I'm sick of seeing these little fiends take over neighborhoods and hurt people. If someone doesn't find a cure soon, I'm afraid humanity will be in trouble. Like, extinction levels of trouble."

That surprised Covie. She knew the plush were a nuisance and getting bolder by the minute. But . . . human extinction? She'd never gone that far in her ruminations. "Really? You think that's a possibility? I mean, yeah, the little buggers are annoying, but they're incredibly dumb and unorganized. What makes you think they'll be able to wipe us out?"

"If I'd known this was going to turn into a lengthy philosophical discussion," he grumbled, dropping the sack of pelts to the ground, then sitting on it, "I would have sat down to begin with." He gestured for Covie to sit across from him.

She sat on the cold tile, a little jealous of Mac's makeshift cushion.

"Is that why you"—Covie waved at his pelt-covered coat—"do that?"

"Yeah. That, and to make a little cash on the side."

Her eyebrows shot up. "Wait. Someone pays you to kill plush?"

"Not exactly." He picked up a piece of broken tile and threw it at the claw machine. It clinked against the glass, then fell to the floor, bouncing a few times before coming to a stop. "After I gut the claw machines—and the plush inside them—I sell the empty machines to the highest bidder."

Covie perked up. Maybe he could help her out. "So . . . you've done this to other claw machines?"

Mac laughed. "Yeah. Lots of them."

Words flooded out of her mouth. "Have you seen a

claw machine with a big purple narwhal sticker, partially scratched off, and a unicorn sticker on the glass?"

"Can't say for sure, but maybe. Why?"

Shoot! Why? Covie couldn't tell him the real reason, not yet anyway. "It's . . . well, I heard anyway . . . that it's important to finding the cure."

"How is it important?" He rested his arm across his bent knee and leaned toward her a little.

Covie shrugged, changing the subject. "Who do you sell these machines to? I mean, what could they even be used for besides their intended purpose?"

"Like I said, I sell them to the highest bidder—and I don't ask what they use them for." The skin around his eye crinkled, again making her think he was smiling under the mask. "I do know what my best customer uses them for, though. And it is true poetic justice."

"Well, are you going to tell me who that is?"

He laughed, a deep, guttural sound. "A plush named Sharkey. He's the warden of a plush prison, and he uses the claw machines as cells for the prisoners."

"Ha!" Covie blurted. "Poetic justice indeed."

"Indeed." Mac nodded.

"So you find the claw machines, remove all the Safe Stuffing plush, *gut* the plush to prevent them from somehow becoming animated, then sell the empty claw machines to the highest bidder."

"Correct."

"What do you do with all the pelts?" Covie nodded to the sack he used as a cushion.

"I add them to my collection. Like an entomologist who pins his catches to corkboards to display."

She cocked an eyebrow. "That's just weird. And gross."

That deep laugh rumbled through the metal beak

again and Mac made a circling motion about his head with a gloved hand. "And what about this *isn't* weird?"

"You've got a point." Covie smiled. She was starting to warm up to this bizarre man.

CHAPTER
TWENTY-FOUR

Covie walked beside Mac, the long strips of plush pelts that made up his coat flowing about him as he stepped. She looked up at him. "So, my weird, metal-masked, vigilante friend. Can I ask you another question?"

"Go for it." He grunted. "But you can just call me Mac."

"Okay, Mac." They stopped at the entrance to the deserted toy store. Apparently, he hadn't bothered with stealth when he'd entered. He'd just smashed his way through the boarded-up glass doors. Covie's boots ground some of the small pieces of glass into the tile. "*Do you remember seeing the claw machine I asked about earlier? The one with the narwhal and unicorn stickers? It was at the Stop a Sec just outside of town a couple of days ago.*"

Mac rested his arm on the metal crossbar of the door and looked up at the ceiling. "I can't say for sure. I sold a few of them to Sharkey yesterday, but I don't remember seeing any stickers on them."

Wondering if finding this Sharkey plush might kill two birds with one stone—he seemed like the kind of character that would know who Plush Zero was, *and* he might be in possession of the claw machine that zapped her—Covie turned on the little girl charm. "Mac"—she opened her eyes wide, going for the innocent child look— "would you take me there, to the plush prison? So I can talk to Sharkey about it?"

"I don't know . . . What about your parents? Won't they be worried about you?"

"I'm an orphan. On my own. No one to answer to," she lied, shaking her head sadly.

"Ah, well, as long as there are no adults to yell at me, I'm in. Let's go."

Shocked at how easy it had been to talk him into it, Covie had to jog to catch up after ducking through the broken door behind him. *Such a strange man*, she thought, watching his multicolored duster sway as he walked.

"How much farther?" Covie's eyes darted all around. The excitement at the possibility of getting some more answers had worn off during the long walk. And now she started to question her sanity. What was she think-ing? Following the strangest person she'd ever met to the farthest reaches of the city. To the deserted outskirts. Trapped in the body of a child. Hadn't she learned any-thing from the night she'd been attacked while sleeping in her car?

"Almost there. Don't start whining now, kid."

"I'm not whining," Covie snapped. "You do realize that I have to take two and a half steps to your every one, though, right? Which means I've essentially walked two-point-five times farther than you."

"*Essentially?*" His one visible eyebrow disappeared

under the top edge of his metal mask as he looked down at her, his eye sparkling with amusement—at least that's what she hoped it was sparkling with. "Were your parents English professors or something?"

"Something like that," she mumbled.

They rounded a dilapidated warehouse building and Mac said, "We're here."

Covie stopped, mouth agape as she stared at the scene before her. It looked like something from a nightmare. Or Chernobyl a few decades after the nuclear meltdown occurred. "What is this place?" she whispered.

"Plush Prison," Mac answered. "Come on."

"Are you serious?"

He didn't answer. He plodded toward a perimeter fence made from welded together chunks of an ancient Ferris wheel. Covie swallowed and followed him, a little bit of admiration peeking out from behind the horror-movie-level dread pooling in her stomach. Whoever had built that Ferris wheel fence had done a good job. Not aesthetically—it was as ugly as the rubble of a war-torn city—but functionally? It worked for security purposes.

Covie's heart pounded in her chest, and she had to stop herself from grabbing Mac's hand out of fear as he stepped onto the tilted porch of the guard house. The thick stripes of paint that had once been colorful but were now faded to a near monochromatic dullness, plus large crooked letters—F-U-N—barely hanging on above the guard's head, let Covie know it had once been a carnival fun house.

"Hey, dude," Mac said to the scroungy bison plush wearing a faded and frayed carnival vest. "We need to talk to the warden."

An armadillo plush, also wearing an old vest, nosed

its way past the bison and looked Mac up and down. "Wasn't you just here yesterday?" It curled its lip up in disgust as it eyed the pelts making up Mac's duster.

"I didn't realize I was only allowed a certain number of visits." Mac leaned toward the plush. "But if you don't let me in to talk to your boss, I'll have to leave here with something else to make my trip worthwhile." He poked a finger at the armadillo, then ran his fingers along the hanging pelts, letting them drop back into place one by one. "I don't have any roly-poly pelts in my collection . . ."

The armadillo squealed and scurried back behind the bison, who looked up at Mac lazily. "I'll take ya to see him. Meet me at the gate." It tipped its head to indicate a tilt-a-whirl car next to the guard house.

The bison disappeared into the dark of the ramshackle building as Mac and Covie stepped over to the "gate." The back of the car faced them, and Mac stood with his hands in his pockets, waiting. Covie looked from him to the tall back of the metal car, the sparse remaining decals cracked and peeling. She jumped as the car jolted, turning toward them with a screech of unoiled parts. She took a breath. Like it or not, she was going in.

CHAPTER
TWENTY-FIVE

The tilt-a-whirl stopped with a clang and Mac stepped into the car, holding on to the arched roof as he stood. "Come on, kid," he said to Covie. "Just don't sit down."

"No kidding." She eyed the fiberglass seat, or what was left of it. It was full of jagged holes exposing the rusted metal frame beneath it. She grabbed the curved metal barrier meant to keep riders from sliding out and stumbled back when the car turned with another jolt. Mac put a steadying hand on her back just long enough for her to get her balance. "Thanks," she said.

Covie's breath caught in her throat as the car completed its rotation and rumbled to a stop. The scattered pieces of carnival equipment spread out before her looked like a pile of junk deposited there by a tornado after it had demolished an amusement park. She stood, staring, for several seconds after Mac had already stepped down from the car-gate.

"You coming?" he asked, already several steps away from her.

"Oh yes, I'm coming." She wiped dirt and rust flakes off her hand onto her sweatpants and followed Mac and the bison plush through a maze of twisted carnival rides and fragments of midway games and food shacks.

They made their way through narrow passages, curved chunks of roller-coaster tracks fencing them in on either side, towering above them, the ride's train-like cars interspersed throughout. Other passages branched out from this main one, each one constructed from a different carnival ride, torn apart and reworked into a functional wall of security. Maybe the random pile of junk she'd first thought it to be actually made sense. There was a method to this madness.

Covie slowed to peer down a passageway constructed of the torn-apart remains of a giant carousel. She hugged herself as a chill sent a tremor from her head to her toes. There had to be dozens of carousel horses, skewered with the thick poles that had never seemed ominous or cruel until this moment. Their partially opened mouths and hand-painted eyes were frozen in screams of silent terror where they hung suspended among the other ripped and shredded pieces of the carousel. Another childhood favorite ruined for life.

Mac grabbed her arm and pulled her away from the passageway roughly. Before she could utter her indignation, he stepped between her and the wooden-horse graveyard, pulling his knife from his belt. "She's off limits, you disgusting, mangy, twisted ball of fur!"

With a squeak, whatever was hidden among the interwoven iron and wood scurried away without revealing itself.

"What . . . what was that? I didn't see anything there." Covie squinted to catch a glimpse of the retreating threat.

Mac replaced his knife in the sheath on his belt and closed his duster over it, then tapped the green lens covering his right eye. "This is a plush-signature reader. My own invention. I can see plush from far away and through solid structures—makes hunting them down much easier."

Covie swallowed, trying to rid her voice of a fearful tremor before speaking. "I bet." Then she went back to her original question. "What was in there?"

He glared down the trail. "Lots of things are in there. The particular thing I warned off is an evil plush octopus and former puppet. You'll see some of its work up ahead, I'm afraid." Without further explanation, he hurried to catch up to the bison.

Covie followed close behind, clutching the handle of her machete, now even more wary of the gloomy passageways. She breathed a sigh of relief when they stepped out into an open area and the sun's rays warmed her face. Her relief was short-lived, however. Before they even reached the large building made up of a crazed architect's nightmares, her arm hair stood at attention and an uneasy sensation crawled just under her skin.

The bison nosed aside the flap of the humongous circus tent that made up a good portion of the patchwork building. Bent and rusting nails and bolts attached the canvas of the tent to a hodgepodge of pieces from other buildings and attached those pieces to each other in a towering, sprawling mess. Bare bulbs dangled from the tall ceiling, casting the interior in an eerie, dim light.

Just inside the door stood a ten-foot-tall clown statue, jagged teeth recently carved into its painted smile, holding a large canvas with the words "WELCOME TO PLUSH PRISON" spray painted in red across its surface. Behind the graffiti, Covie could still make out the original painting, though faded and filthy, of misshapen human forms and animals with two heads or other physical anomalies. "Freak Show 5¢" was emblazoned across the top.

"This way, humans," the bison guard said. "Don't touch anything."

Mac took a deep breath and rubbed the back of his neck, hesitating just a moment before following the guard.

Covie caught up to him and whispered, "Do you trust this Sharkey?"

He shrugged. "I don't know. He pays well."

"Great," she mumbled under her breath.

They passed through a curtained partition, ratty with rips and tears, into the center of the circus tent. On either side of them, towers of claw machines rose to the top. A crane with a giant claw stacked the machines one on top of another.

"Fitting," Covie said.

The room was huge and unorganized. Snarling plush clawed and spit on the inside of the plexiglass coverings of their new jail cells.

Covie perked up and stepped closer to the ones nearest her, looking for the narwhal and unicorn stickers among the dented, paint-chipped, scratched machines. Focused on the outside of the machines, she screamed and jumped back, falling on her butt, when something slammed up against the plexiglass from inside—the thin barrier the only thing between the unholy creature trapped inside, and Covie's face.

She scrambled backward, not even bothering to try to stand. "What in the deuces is that thing?"

Mac reached a hand out to help her up. "That is a hush. Part human, part plush—but mostly plush." He nodded at the creature with a human torso and a plush gorilla head and limbs. "That's what that vile octopus plush wanted you for."

CHAPTER
TWENTY-SIX

Covie grabbed Mac's hand and he helped her up. He tried to pull his hand away, but she clung to it like a lifeline as she stared at the raging hush. He allowed her to retain her grip on him, but urged her away from the claw machine. "Come on, kid. The bison is getting ahead of us."

She turned her head to continue staring as he dragged her to follow the guard. "Why is it just screaming and flailing like that?"

Mac shook his head. "Whatever the mad scientist octopus does to attach the human parts messes with the sentience of the plush. They turn into rabid, mindless monstrosities."

"Why haven't you killed it? The octopus? Or why isn't it locked up, at least?"

His grip on her hand tightened and his voice came out rough, angry. "I can't kill any plush here—it's an agreement between me and Sharkey. And Sharkey *did* have it locked up, but the blasted thing is an escape artist. The only intelligent plush, and it has to be insanely evil." He let go of her hand and she let him pull it away this time. "But I'll get it," he whispered. "I'll really enjoy pulling its stuffing out slowly while it screams. I just have to catch it outside the perimeter of the prison."

The bison stopped at a metal door and turned to them. "Wait here. I'll see if he's in."

Covie's eyes roamed, warily checking out the prisoners in the claw machine cells. At least two of the plush repeatedly leaped to grab the claw hanging above them, then swung, crashing their soft feet into the plexiglass, trying to break it. They really were dumb creatures. Most of them. She shuddered, thinking about the octopus mad scientist.

Several of the cells had more than one plush in them. Three at the most, that she could see. Some of them banged on the glass, shouting obscenities. Some just sat, slumped against the glass, despondent and silent.

The bison guard came back out and glanced suspiciously at Covie before speaking to Mac. "He isn't too thrilled about the girl being here, but he'll let her come in with you, Mac, as long as you do the talking. He don't want to talk to her."

Mac looked at Covie and raised his eyebrow out of sight beneath the mask. "I think I need to hear this story." He turned to the guard. "Okay, I'll do the talking."

The warden's office was surprisingly . . . *normal human* looking. The plush warden sat in a tall chair behind a desk overflowing with papers. The dolphin plush only had one eye and made no attempts to cover up the gaping hole where the other one used to be. Tufts of purulent stuffing poked out of it. Multiple bald spots dappled its gray fur. Its lower jaw was crooked and didn't line up with the top jaw. Covie tried not to stare when it spoke, its battered jaw moving side-to-side instead of up and down. "Have a seat."

Mac and Covie sat in chairs across the desk from the warden.

"So, Mac," Sharkey said, refusing to even acknowledge Covie's presence, "I'm surprised to see you again so soon. I just purchased a couple of machines from you yesterday. Why are you gracing us with your presence again?"

"I'm trying to find a specific claw machine that has a partially scratched-off purple narwhal sticker and a unicorn sticker up on the glass."

"What's so special about this machine?" the sideways-talking dolphin asked.

"Nothing, really. It'll just help me out with an investigation I'm doing. If you have it, I'll swap it out for a better one."

The plush warden tapped a fin on its desk and stared at Mac in silence.

Covie held in a sigh. Going nonstop the last several days was catching up to her, and her eyelids were growing heavy. She occupied herself by studying the paperwork on Sharkey's desk. Leaning forward, she caught sight of one particular piece of paper—a small corner of it anyway—that contained something that perked her right up: PATIENT ZERO, written in all caps.

Sharkey sighed, apparently losing the one-eyed staring contest with Mac, and shrugged. "I have no idea. You're the only one I get these machines from. Wouldn't you know if you'd sold me this *special* one?"

Mac shook his head. "I don't remember seeing it. It's not like I inspect them before bringing them in, Sharkey."

How could Covie see the rest of that paper? She tapped her fingers on her thigh. She didn't want to do anything to ruin Mac's business relationship with Sharkey, but she really needed to see what it said.

"I'll tell you what," Sharkey said, "you have my permission to go look for it. I won't have time to go with you. We caught a handful of Window's gang. You know he got murdered?" For the first time since they'd entered the office, the dolphin glanced Covie's way. "Just take the girl with you . . . and keep an eye on her."

Covie looked away. *Does he know I did it?*

Mac nodded. "Thanks, Warden. Will do."

The dolphin slid off its chair and waddled to the door, Mac right behind it. Covie stood, looked at the warden jumping to reach the door handle, and grabbed the paper from the desk. All it said was "PATIENT ZERO," with an address under it. She memorized the address and then tucked the paper back where it had been before following Mac and the dolphin out the door.

CHAPTER
TWENTY-SEVEN

Sharkey led Covie and Mac back to the cell area and snapped at the guards, "These two have my permission to look around. Don't hassle them."

"Yes, boss," said a sloth plush with a taser strapped around its waist.

The other two guards just nodded, stealing angry glances at Covie. She smiled at them and placed her hand on the hilt of her machete. They both backed away.

Sharkey left them to explore, going back to his office.

"Which side of the machine were the stickers on?" Mac asked her.

"The side with the prize drawer, near the pink Safe Stuffing sticker."

He nodded and walked along a row of cells, looking quickly up each stack before moving to the next. Covie started doing the same across the aisle from him. The tall stacks of claw machines swayed back and forth precariously, adding one more reason to hurry besides her desire to investigate that address she'd seen. *Patient Zero, not Plush Zero. What could that mean?*

They rushed to finish their search, neither of them finding Covie's claw machine.

＊ ＊ ＊

Mac walked back to the city with her, questioning her about her infamous run-in with the now-deceased Window. She told him the basics, leaving out anything to do with Tom—that would have been too hard to explain. Eleven-year-olds didn't have husbands.

Mac nodded and slapped her on the back with a grin. "You are a stud." He pulled his duster to the side and reached for something hanging at the back of his belt. Producing a good-sized knife in a black sheath, he handed it to her. "That there's a Bowie knife. If you're going to be doing dangerous things, you need to have at least two weapons at your disposal. Keep it on you at all times."

Aww. The big weird guy had a soft spot for her. She smiled and thanked him, sliding the knife into her boot, clipping its sheath to the top of it.

When they neared the center of the city, Mac stopped and looked at her. "Well, kid, it's been a pleasure hanging out with you today, but I have work to do. Now that the Safe Stuffing formula has been released, I'm on a time crunch to find all the claw machines and rid the world of plush before they all become animated. And I need to go get my truck so I can pick up the machine we emptied at the toy store earlier. See ya around." He turned and jogged away.

"Wait!" Covie yelled, hurrying to catch up to him.

He stopped and glared down at her.

"If you find the claw machine—the one I'm looking for—can you somehow let me know?"

Mac sighed and thought for a minute. "Yeah. Gimme your phone."

She dug it out of her pocket, unlocked the screen,

and handed it to him. He put his number in her contacts, texted himself so he'd have hers, then gave it back to her.

Before he could jog off again, Covie had one more question. With a scowl on her face she said, "And . . . you have a *truck*? Why did we *walk* all the way to the plush prison if you have a truck?"

He laughed and shook his head, saying over his shoulder as he jogged off again, "Think about it, kid. Grown man, little girl. Getting in a beater truck. Doesn't look good."

She stared after him, mouth agape. The weirdo wearing a metal plague-doctor mask and a duster made out of plush pelts was worried about his reputation? At least her excuse for not telling him about her car was solid—little girls didn't have cars. It might have been funny if her feet and legs didn't hurt so bad.

"On that note . . ." she mumbled as she turned toward where she'd left her car that morning, her backpack digging into her shoulders. As tired as she felt, it was hard to believe it was only early afternoon. She pulled the keys out of her pocket and unlocked her car, determined not to let exhaustion slow down her quest.

Patient Zero.

She had an address.

Covie slung the backpack into the passenger seat and sat on her cushion that made it so she could drive. She locked the doors and rested her head against the back of the seat, closing her eyes for only a few seconds—worried that any longer and she'd fall asleep. With a sigh, she dug through the backpack and pulled out a granola bar and a bottle of water. She plugged her phone in to charge and wolfed down the scant food before starting the car.

Repeating the address from the paper she'd found on Sharkey's desk, she drove to an area of the city she'd never been to before. She parked a few blocks from where her presumed destination was and went the rest of the way on foot. She had no idea what to expect and could be much more stealthy on foot—even though the last thing she wanted to do right now was walk even more.

The closer she got to the address, the more she thought that maybe she'd remembered it wrong. She stayed off the pothole-filled road, walking in the tall grass next to it, hidden amongst the shadows of trees and boarded-up buildings. The area was deserted. Even for a place where plush had taken over. She stopped, gazing ahead at what should have been the building attached to the address she'd memorized. Maybe she'd gotten it wrong. The old military hospital had boarded-up windows and graffiti spray painted all over the exterior.

Covie snuck closer, stooping down to push through a chain-link fence someone had cut through. A car drove around from the back of the building, and she ducked behind the tall weeds next to the fence, peeking through the leaves. A big plush German shepherd was at the wheel of a black BMW sedan.

That looks like Charlotte's car, Covie thought as it got closer. Odd. *Did they get Charlotte?! I hope she's okay.*

She had no idea what Charlotte's license plate number was, but she pulled her phone out and took a picture of it as it drove past her, wondering if she was just being paranoid. Why would Char's car be here? But it *really* looked like her car. Covie would check it later—when she had time. She had a sudden surge of adrenaline, needing not only to find Patient Zero, but make sure her friend was safe.

CHAPTER
TWENTY-EIGHT

Avoiding the side of the building that had crumbled in on itself, Covie snuck into the hospital, hand on the hilt of her machete. She was glad she'd taped the sheath back to her leg so that the machete stayed in easy reach. She stepped lightly, not wanting her footsteps to echo in the empty hallways. Not a soul was around, neither human nor plush.

She shook her head as she weaved around to avoid a stained mattress lying in the middle of the lobby. She headed down the main hallway, her feet crunching on packages of bandages, empty blood tubes, and syringes spilled all over the floor from a tipped-over wire shelving unit. It was like a hospital obstacle course. Covie climbed over a metal gurney tipped on its side as she turned down a different hallway, cautiously checking each room as she went.

Nothing. No claw machine. No Patient Zero. No Plush Zero. And no Char. *Why did Sharkey have this address on his desk?*

Covie righted a tipped-over exam stool and plopped down on it. She'd wasted half a day on this stupid false lead. She huffed out a frustrated breath. Now what? She slid off the stool, deciding to go back to the city to try to find another claw machine on the list in the notebook.

Which way had she come in? She'd gotten turned around during her search. She looked up to where exit signs usually hung. There were some in the intersection of hallways, but they all pointed in different directions. Well, there was more than one way to enter or exit a hospital. She picked a direction and clomped down the hallway. It took her a moment to realize this one wasn't cluttered with junk like the others. She slowed her steps and narrowed her eyes, staring down the darkened corridor. Light flooded out of a doorway about twenty yards down.

Covie pressed up against the wall on the same side the light came from. She crept toward it. A steady beep grew louder the closer she got. She stopped and held her breath, looking both ways down the corridor. She strained to hear any noise coming from the room or anywhere nearby. Nothing but the rhythmic beeping. She slowly let out her breath, then crept to the edge of the open door.

The odor of disinfectant cleaner pierced her nose, along with other, even less pleasant smells, as she peeked into the room, hand on her machete and heart rate spiking. A large tan plush bear stood still—as if at attention for a military inspection—in front of a closed hospital curtain. Covie figured the plush to be about five feet tall— for sure taller than her hopefully-temporary child body. She observed the motionless bear from behind for several minutes before deciding it either wasn't animated or had somehow been paused or turned off like a battery-operated toy.

When she was relatively certain the plush was immobilized somehow, she edged farther into the trash-strewn room to get a look at its front side. Covie gasped and slapped her hand over her mouth.

The plush bear's mouth had been sewn shut with thick blue thread crisscrossing its lips. Medical tubes of all types protruded from different areas of its body. Thick, scab-colored corrugated plastic tubing came from a slit in its throat and was attached to a large green metal cylinder. She retched at the sight of a clear tube about the diameter of her thumb, draining a pale yellow sludge from the bear's chest down into a see-through rectangular box taped to the floor at its feet. Another gag escaped her throat when her gaze reached several bulb-shaped drains inserted into its abdomen, each one partially full of pea-green or muddy-brown fluid. IV tubing ran from opaque bags hanging on a metal pole into both arms of the plush.

Covie stepped closer to the bear, taking in its worn and ragged plush fur. Her eyes widened and she swallowed down a surprised curse—a pulsating cord the size, shape, and color of an umbilical cord ran from the plush's belly down to the floor, disappearing under the hospital curtain.

A thought slammed into her as she looked up at the sleeping or comatose bear—was this Plush Zero? Had she found the plush she'd been searching for? The one that had been infected and animated first?

She reached out a shaking hand to touch the worn fur on its arm. It was mangy and crusted, but the cloth beneath it was warm. The plush didn't stir at her touch.

The pulsating umbilical cord drew her gaze back. Covie crouched, following it to the worn tile. She got down on her hands and knees and crawled under the curtain, tracking it to the side of a bed and up . . .

"Holy crap!" She slapped her hand over her mouth again, unable to keep the words inside this time.

A human boy lay in the old, rusting hospital bed.

CHAPTER
TWENTY-NINE

Frozen in fear that someone—or some*thing*—heard her outcry, Covie crouched next to the bed, waiting to be found. Her heart rate slowed after a minute of no discovery. She stood, taking in the tattered, worn sheets and blanket covering the boy. The umbilical cord disappeared beneath the blanket.

Covie watched the boy's chest rise and fall, relieved he was breathing. Her mind was having trouble processing the whole thing. Where was that umbilical cord going? After another glance at the sleeping boy, she lifted the blanket, shaking her head to see the cord inserted and sewn into a swollen red slit in the boy's belly button, above a worn pair of pajama pants.

The boy and the plush bear were connected by the umbilical cord.

She dropped the blanket and picked up an old yellowed paper chart that hung at the foot of the bed. Stamped on the front of the chart in red letters were the words "PATIENT ZERO."

The bear on the other side of the curtain *had* to be Plush Zero. Covie was certain of it.

With shaky hands, she flipped open the chart. The

name at the top was Oliver Connelly. She frowned. Same as Charlotte's last name.

It had to be just a coincidence.

Covie would have *known* if her best friend had a son!

Just an odd coincidence, that was all.

She stared at the chart, her mind going back to the car she saw leaving as she stooped by the fence. The car that had looked like Charlotte's. She shook her head, freeing the nagging feeling. What was she thinking? Char was her best friend.

The boy rested peacefully, the beeping of the heart machine a strangely soothing background noise. Covie looked up at the ancient monitor. A reflection flickered across the screen—the bear, its head through the curtain, staring at her.

Before she could spin around, it grabbed her backpack and pulled her away from Oliver. The curtain tore with a quick succession of loud rips as the grommets split one by one. The bear flung her across the trash-littered floor. She looked up at the plush as she slid to a stop. It jumped into the air, agile as a cat, and Covie rolled to the left a split second before it landed where she'd just been.

The bear raised a foot to slam down on her, and she rolled again, this time *toward* the filthy plush, taking out the leg it stood on. It tumbled down on top of her in a tangle of fur and medical tubes. The IV pole crashed onto the ground next to them, still connected to the tubing in the bear's arms. The tube in its chest ripped free, spraying Covie with the thick, yellow, putrid-smelling sludge.

The plush pushed up onto its hands and knees above her. She brought her bent knees to her chest and planted her feet square in its gut, kicking up to push the bear off her. It grunted as it slammed into the foot of the bed. Covie jumped to her feet, shook off the backpack, letting it drop to the floor, and pulled the machete from its sheath at her side.

Goo still leaked from the hole where the chest tube had been as the bear gained its feet and barreled toward Covie. She hacked at its neck with the machete, cutting through the corrugated tubing, but only striking a minor scratch to the plush's neck. She jumped against the wall as the bear swung at her, missing as the IV tubing stretched to its maximum distance, holding the bear back.

It looked down at the restraining tubes and ripped them out of its arms. The bear charged her, and she bolted toward the door, but the plush beat her there and slammed it shut. She swung the machete, striking a blow to its chest. Bloody stuffing sprayed from the gash, all over Covie, the wall, and the floor.

The wounded plush lowered its shoulder and took two running steps, crashing into her, sending them both rocketing into the big metal tank, the corrugated tubing flapping back and forth as it released whatever gas it contained. Her breath whooshed from her lungs as she and the bear both toppled to the ground along with the tank— Covie to the left and the bear to the right. The machete clanged to the ground as well, sliding out of her reach.

On her hands and knees, Covie struggled to draw in a breath, chest muscles spasming and sharp pains stabbing her ribs. Intent on reinflating her lungs, she didn't notice the plush moving toward her. She finally gulped a lungful of air just as the bear wrapped its arms around her torso and arms, lifting her off the ground.

Able to take in a couple more breaths, she kicked at the plush as it held her with her back against its chest, her arms pinned to her sides. Sticky, wet liquid squelched against her back. The stench of bloody stuffing and old ratty plush hair stung her nostrils, and she had to swallow down the bile creeping up her throat. She struggled against the plush bear, kicking and throwing her head back, hoping to make contact.

The bear's violent embrace tightened against her battered ribs, making it difficult to breathe. She had to do something. Had to get away from this plush. The more she fought, the tighter it squeezed.

Covie looked down, barely able to inhale more than a gulp of air. The umbilical cord hung near her ankles. She fought harder, going in and out of consciousness.

CHAPTER THIRTY

Gritting her teeth, Covie strained with all her might, wishing for the millionth time that she had her strong, defined adult muscles to fight with. She freed her right arm from the plush bear's cinch and reached for the Bowie knife in her boot, pulling it out with the tips of her fingers. She bobbled it and lost her grip, but caught it before it fell out of her reach. Holding the knife with a firm grip, Covie lifted the umbilical cord with her foot, grasping it in her left hand beneath the bear's constricting hold, which still pinned her left arm to her side.

Using the Bowie knife, she sawed back and forth against the thick rubber-like tissue of the umbilical cord while her lungs burned for oxygen. The plush's arms tightened, and Covie could no longer draw in even a tiny breath. She had to keep going. She had to sever the stupid cord.

Fluid spurted out as the blade cut through the first layer, giving her hope that she'd made some progress, but making the knife's grip slippery with blood. The knuckles of her hand ached from clutching so tightly to the handle.

Covie continued to saw away at the umbilical cord as her body starved for oxygen. Black dots formed in her vision. Her lips grew numb. Her eyelids grew heavy, but she forced them open with thoughts of Emily and Tom.

The blade cut through the last bit of the cord and she dropped both to the ground, her muscles no longer obeying commands from her oxygen-deprived brain. Covie slumped forward in the bear's arms and tried one last time to inhale. She barely registered the small movement of air into her lungs, but the blackness swimming before her eyes began to dissipate.

The first thing she saw when her vision returned was blood flowing all over the floor from the severed umbilical cord. Was it the plush bear's blood? Or was it Oliver's? The bear relaxed its grip, its movements slow and drawn out. A rustling noise from the bed gained Covie's attention as she gulped in lungfuls of air. Oliver thrashed about, the blanket tangled up around his torso.

Covie shoved the nearly immobile plush's arms away from her and dropped to the floor. Her feet slid out from under her when they hit the blood still leaking from the cord. She stood, holding on to the foot of the bed for balance, and hurried to the boy's side. The blanket was a twisted mess, and blood seeped through it from Oliver's abdominal area. Hands shaking as she continued to breathe too rapidly, Covie untangled the thin, ratty blanket from around the boy and ripped the umbilical cord out of his belly, clamping the bundled-up portion of the blanket to the bleeding wound. "Oliver?"

The boy continued to thrash with his eyes closed while she held pressure with the blanket. The plush bear had fallen to the ground unnoticed by her while Covie had been tending to the boy. A throaty growl caught her attention, and she whirled to face whom she still thought was Plush Zero. It crawled toward her. She stepped back as it reached for her foot, its plastic eyes glaring at her, its mouth working beneath the crisscrossed thread restraining it.

Plush Zero wants this boy, she thought. *He must be really important to this whole plushdemic thing.*

Covie kicked the bear in the head several times, scooting it back across the bloody floor, away from Oliver. She needed to get the boy out of here. She searched the room, her gaze landing on a wheelchair in the darkened, unused side of the hospital room. She looked from the wheelchair back to the boy, then around the room again. He wasn't awake. He wouldn't be able to assist in their escape. Maybe she should just leave him here. Abandon him.

She shook her head. No way. She couldn't do that.

With another shove to push the still-crawling bear away from the bed, Covie darted out into the hallway. She ran to the tipped-over supply cart and grabbed a roll of gauze, a package of square gauze, and some surgical tape before returning to the bloody room.

The wheelchair was covered in dust, and Covie fleetingly worried about Oliver's wound getting infected before deciding that was the least of their worries. She pushed the chair over to the side of the bed, straining to get it over the garbage littering the floor. The side rail on the bed stuck. Covie kicked it several times before it unlatched and fell below the level of the thin mattress. Her ribs screamed, sharp pain stabbing through her chest and back as she heaved the boy off the bed and roughly plopped him in the wheelchair. He was about the same height as her, maybe even a little taller, but he weighed less, she guessed, from the looks of his pasty skin and skeletal body.

Covie ripped the top off the square-gauze package

and took them all out, shoving them against the hole in Oliver's belly. She held it in place by wrapping the whole roll of gauze around him multiple times.

The bear inched around the foot of the bed and reached for Oliver's foot. Covie jerked the chair back out of its reach, and the boy slumped forward, nearly toppling out of the seat. She caught him by the shoulder and pulled him against the cracked faux-leather back.

She wiped the sweat off her forehead with the sleeve of her T-shirt and cursed under her breath. Hoping she'd moved far enough away from the plush to buy a few seconds, Covie used the surgical tape to secure the unconscious Oliver to the wheelchair, wrapping it around his chest and arms and the backrest of the chair.

This wheelchair was definitely not built for four-wheeling, she thought as she struggled to push it over the medical trash on the floor. She pulled it back, trying for another angle, only to have it jolt to a stop when one of the front wheels hit the drooping corrugated tubing.

With a grunt, Covie shoved the wheelchair, running over the plush bear's outstretched hand, and finally made it to the hallway with the moaning, slumped-over Oliver.

CHAPTER
THIRTY-ONE

Covie leaned against the wall, holding on to the handles of the wheelchair as she caught her breath. She couldn't just leave Plush Zero alive to disappear again.

Plus, she'd left her weapons in there. And the backpack.

With a sigh, she whispered, "I'll be right back, Oliver." She straightened her shoulders and marched back into the room to finish off the bear she was sure was Plush Zero.

Knowing she needed to completely gut the five-foot-tall plush in order to kill it, she almost talked herself out of it. She was exhausted and in pain—no one would blame her for leaving it to someone else.

She stepped over the struggling legs of the plush bear and retrieved her machete, wiping the blood stuffing off the blade with a bed sheet before returning it to the sheath fastened to her leg. The Bowie knife took more of a search effort to find. After looking all around the area where she'd dropped it, including under the bed, Covie turned to the bear, lying face down as it tried to reach her. She sighed, then heaved the plush over onto its back. The knife Mac had given her lay next to the gore-covered bear. She picked it up with two fingers, not wanting to touch

the nasty fluid that had come from the umbilical cord—
then she realized the nasty goo was already all over her.
Shaking her head at herself, she cleaned the handle and
blade as well as she could, then turned to the plush bear.

Maybe she should try to get some information out
of it before de-stuffing it. She knelt next to it and tilted
her head as she watched it feebly reach for her with an
angry crease in the worn fur of its forehead. With the tip
of the knife, Covie sliced through the thread sewn across
its mouth. It stretched its maw and emitted a low growl.

"Where is the claw machine that was at the Stop a
Sec? The booby-trapped one." Covie held the knife where
the bear could see it. Plush Zero had to know where it
was—Window's goons had said he was the one boo-
by-trapping them.

The plush bear clamped its mouth shut again, glaring
at her.

"We can do this the easy way, in which you just
answer my questions, or the hard way." She wiggled the
knife in front of its eyes.

Still nothing from the plush.

"Look"—Covie pushed the tip of the knife against
the fur just under its left eye—"I'm really not a sadistic
torturer. I find it repulsive, actually. But I'm tired of being
stuck in this child body, and frankly, I'm tired of you
devious, evil plush trying to ruin the world. Now either
tell me where that claw machine is, or I'm going to cut
this eye out of your head."

The plush's mouth twisted into a toothless smile, but
it didn't utter a word.

*Either it thinks I'm bluffing, or it's insane enough not
to care what I do to it,* Covie thought. She shrugged and
tried not to cringe as she dug the knife under the hard plastic eye and half pried and half sliced it off the bear's face.

The bear writhed and tried to pull away, reaching for her knife hand. She knocked its grubby plush paw away and pinned it to the floor with her knee. "Where is the claw machine?"

Bloody stuffing oozed out of the eyehole like Play-Doh squeezing from an ice cream set. The plush remained silent.

After a couple more plunges of the knife, Covie gave up. Either the stupid bear didn't know, couldn't talk, or just plain wasn't willing to tell her. She set to work killing the plush, starting by cutting its head off. She gagged as she reached inside the pelt to remove the blood stuffing; the stench pouring off this plush seemed ten times worse than the others.

Covie scooped up some of the stuffing and put it in an old bag for patient belongings, sealing it with the surgical tape so the odor couldn't escape. She'd deliver the sample to Tom so he and the other scientists could use it to hopefully find a cure to this plushdemic.

She rinsed her hands and arms off in a filthy sink in the room. The water running from the tap was a rusty brown color, but it was better than the gore from gutting Plush Zero. She looked back at the scattered bloody stuffing and ripped pelt and wondered if she should do something with it other than just leave it lying about. How likely was it that an unanimated plush would come in contact with the contagious stuffing? Not very, she decided. The hospital was deserted and falling to pieces. Who would bring a child's toy to this place?

Anyway, she figured most of the plush without Safe Stuffing had already been turned, so it wasn't worth the effort to haul it out and get rid of it.

She nodded once to herself, certain she was right.

CHAPTER
THIRTY-TWO

Covie maneuvered the wheelchair out of the building with some difficulty, often needing to stop and move things out of the way in order to get it past the trash and clutter. She'd hung her backpack and bag of stuffing on the chair's handles, too tired to carry them. Pain shot through her ribs with any amount of exertion from where Plush Zero had tackled her into the metal container and then tried to squeeze the life out of her. Something was probably broken.

"I need to get you to a real hospital," she said to the unconscious boy.

By the time she reached the car she'd parked blocks away, Oliver was completely out again, not even moaning as he slumped against the surgical tape. Covie leaned against the car for a few minutes to catch her breath, thinking about her next move. She needed a safe place to hide—for her and Oliver. She examined the abdominal dressing she'd applied to his wounded belly, relieved to see that the bleeding seemed to have stopped. First-aid supplies were added to her mental list.

She sighed and opened the back passenger door of her car, then unwound the tape from around Oliver and the back of the wheelchair. With a grunt of pain and exertion, she lifted his limp body under his arms and pivoted with him, dumping him clumsily into the back seat. The seat belt barely stretched far enough to latch around the awkwardly positioned boy.

She dropped the backpack into the front passenger seat and the smelly bag of plush stuffing into the trunk, then turned to the wheelchair.

Folding it turned out to be a chore. The parts were all rusted and stuck from disuse. A huge number of curse words and several kicks to the jammed pieces finally did the trick. Covie heaved the now-folded wheelchair into the trunk and slammed it shut.

Her tired limbs rejoiced as she settled into the driver's seat.

Covie's stomach growled. Add food to the list. And water.

She had no idea where she would find any of those things, but first things first. Hunger gnawed at her guts now that the adrenaline had run its course, so she leaned forward and started the car, turned the headlights on in the waning daylight, and pulled out onto the crumbling road.

Oliver lay sleeping in the back seat while Covie studied him in the rearview mirror.

Who is this kid? I have so many questions to ask him. And if I take him to the hospital, what will happen to me? I'd have to justify why a little girl drove an emaciated kid to the hospital. I have no way of explaining that, and they'd want to call my parents. I'd have to stay, and that would ruin my chances to find the claw machine.

Covie looked at the bandage on his belly, feeling guilty. How could she be so selfish?

But maybe the hospital can wait until he wakes up

and I can at least ask him some questions first. He doesn't seem like he needs to go to the emergency room.

She pushed the guilt way down inside and justified that she could wait till he woke up, then take him to the hospital. It wasn't the most responsible thing a mother could do, but she started to feel okay about her decision to wait.

She'd passed an abandoned grocery store on her way to the military facility, and headed in that direction, hoping to find at least some of the things she needed.

Parking near the entrance, the double glass doors shattered and hanging askew, Covie checked that the machete and Bowie knife were tucked safely into their respective sheaths, shoved the car keys into her pocket, checked to make sure Oliver was still breathing, and locked the car doors before stepping over the crushed glass to enter the store.

Using the flashlight app on her phone, Covie searched the dark, ransacked store for usable items. The sound of a package being ripped open followed by noisy crunching sent Covie into a crouch behind a tipped-over shelving unit. She struggled to turn the flashlight off; the beam of light bounced around her as she poked at different buttons on her phone.

"Hey!" a gruff voice yelled. "Who's there? That you, Slimy?"

"Huh? What're you talking about? I'm over here," another loud voice said from the back of the store.

Covie sighed. She was so sick of plush. She shoved her phone in her pocket and stood as soon as padded footsteps rushed toward her, pulling the machete out and brandishing it in front of her.

An alligator plush scuttled around the shelves, skidding to a stop a few yards away from her. It looked over its shoulder and yelled, "Hey, Slimy! It's a girl. And she has a sword. Get up here."

Covie didn't wait for the alligator's backup to get there. She sliced the machete through the creature's neck, severing its head from its body. A huge, dirty earthworm plush slunk toward her, and as she stomped to meet it with the sharp blade in her hands, she thought, *Why on Earth would anyone want a stuffed worm?* She chopped it into a dozen pieces, her growing animosity against all things plush fogging her mind momentarily.

Standing over the blood and stuffing guts, she breathed heavily, each inhale sending a sharp pain through her ribs. The pieces of the plush worm continued to wiggle and squirm at her feet, prompting her to finish the job by tearing the stuffing out of the pieces until nothing was left but a pile of bloody gore and shredded plush fur. She moved over to the beheaded alligator and did the same. Double bagging some heavy-duty garbage bags she found still sitting unopened on a shelf, she shoved all the stuffing inside and tied the top. That would have to do to keep the contagious mess away from yet-to-be-infected plush—if there even were any.

Convinced now that she was alone in the abandoned store, Covie rummaged through the sparse items that remained. Six cans of Vienna sausages, a bag of marshmallows, several cans of mandarin oranges and other assorted canned fruit, and a box of knock-off Cheerios made it into her "shopping bag." The stack of anchovies did not make the cut—she wasn't that hungry. There was no bottled water to be found, but she did find a single bottle of Pedialyte—which she celebrated with a loud, "Score!" and a fist pump.

Duct tape and feminine napkins would have to substitute for first-aid supplies, since there was nothing left in the pharmacy area of the store but a dented box of children's bandages. And beneath a fallen stack of vitamins, she found the holy grail—a package of baby wipes. She added the items to another bag, then hauled them out to the car and put them in the back seat with a still-sleeping Oliver.

She was grateful she didn't have to use her credit card. Who knew if the plush could track credit card transactions?

Now to find somewhere safe to camp out for the night.

CHAPTER
THIRTY-THREE

Driving through the deserted suburb, Covie wondered how things had gotten so bad so quickly. All because of furry little stuffed *toys*. People had been forced to leave their homes and abandon their towns after being overrun by the evil creatures.

Exhaustion dragged her eyelids down, her head bobbing as she swerved into a curb with a bump. Her eyes flew open and she jerked the wheel, tires screeching as the car careened back to the center of the fractured road.

"Maybe I'd better just pull over and chance sleeping on the side of the road." She glanced back at Oliver, still breathing but otherwise unmoving. The memory of the last time she'd pulled over to sleep crept into her mind and she shook her head, her stomach rolling with sudden nausea.

The car's headlights illuminated a sign off to her left: Monument High School—Home of the Piranhas. Graffiti nearly covered the picture of the toothy, ferocious-looking fish.

"High school, it is." Cove sighed, turning into the dark parking lot. She pulled around to the side, where an automotive-class garage sat near crumbling tennis courts.

She stopped and put the car in park, then searched her surroundings before getting out. Nothing moved in the shadows around her, so she chanced exiting the vehicle.

The garage door opened with a screech of metal as she pushed it up, the springs taking it from her grasp as it opened the rest of the way. She flipped a light switch, giggling with exaggerated joy when the overhead light flickered to life. A cursory glance showed the space to be empty of human or plush, so Covie pulled the car in and shut it off. She jumped and grabbed the cord attached to the garage door, using her weight to get it moving back down its tracks. She twisted the lock on the handle, then jammed a broom through the handle of the regular door as an extra precaution.

She leaned against the door for a moment, finally able to relax a little. The scent of her own body odor mixed with all the goop, blood, and gore that covered her wafted about, much more obvious now that things were calm. Covie wrinkled her nose and looked around the garage, spotting a restroom sign on a door that was partially ajar.

The bathroom wasn't too disgusting, considering that teenage boys had probably been the main users of the facility. And the toilet still flushed. Covie rinsed off in the sink and studied herself in the mirror. She had a gash in her cheek she didn't remember getting, and when she washed the dried blood off it, it started bleeding again. Holding a paper towel to her face, she returned to the car to grab the bag of makeshift first-aid supplies.

She scowled into the mirror as she applied a third bandage, emblazoned with yellow smiley faces, to the cut on her cheek. The cheap adhesive wasn't strong enough to keep the wound closed, so Covie ripped off a strip of duct tape and plastered it over the top of the bandages, knowing she would regret the decision when the time came to remove it.

Wishing she had another set of clothes to change into, she wiped herself down with baby wipes to get the worst of the grunge off.

Now, what to do with Oliver. She stared at him as he lay in what seemed a very uncomfortable position in the back seat of her car. She wouldn't be able to access and take care of his belly wound like that. Wanting nothing more than to sleep for, like, two days straight, Covie's motherly instincts forced her into action. She wrestled the wheelchair out of the trunk and forced it to unfold, then she struggled to get Oliver out of the car and into it.

She pressed her arm against her injured ribs, wishing she had a bottleful of oxycodone or a vial of morphine. She'd always been adamant about not polluting her fit body with narcotics before, but she'd take some now. Heck, she'd settle for some ibuprofen.

Oliver was already slumped over, slipping from the wheelchair. Covie lunged, grabbing him by the shoulders just in time. She gently repositioned him, then used the duct tape to support him in a sitting position, wrapping it around his chest, lower legs, and arms, securing him to the wheelchair.

He slept through the whole ordeal. Covie wondered what kinds of drugs they'd been pumping into him through that umbilical cord. She shuddered at the thought of blood and fluids flowing from the revolting plush bear into the young boy.

Positioning Oliver right next to the driver's side door, Covie sat in the seat and rolled the window down so she could hear him if he awoke. She ate a full can of Vienna sausages and had marshmallows and Cheerios for dessert. She'd never live it down if the other trainers at the gym ever found out. But her body needed glucose, carbs, and protein to recover from the day's fight-or-flight activities. She washed it all down with several swigs of berry-flavored Pedialyte, then reclined her seat and closed her eyes.

As tired as she was, her mind wasn't ready for sleep just yet, as it replayed the highlight reel from the day. Covie smiled, ecstatic that she'd killed Plush Zero. The smile turned to a tight-lipped scowl as she made plans for tomorrow. Priority number one: She needed to figure out where that claw machine disappeared to. Then she needed to go home and see Tom and Emily and tell them all that had happened. She dozed, exhaustion finally winning the battle.

CHAPTER THIRTY-FOUR

Grunting noises and coughing followed by hoarse but loud yelling brought Covie out of her slumber.

"Where am I?!" Oliver struggled against the duct tape, rocking the wheelchair side-to-side. "Get this stuff off me! Help!"

His head jerked around to glare at her as she opened the car door. "Calm down. It's okay," Covie said in a soothing little-girl voice.

"The heck it is!" Oliver's face was red and beaded with sweat. The veins in his neck bulged as he pulled against the duct tape restraints. "Let me go!"

"Dude, chill." Covie held up her hands as she stepped toward him. "I can't undo the tape while you're bucking like a deranged bull on crack!"

That stopped his convulsion-like battle against the tape, at least temporarily. He stared at her with a half-open mouth for several seconds before pulling against his bonds with renewed vigor. "Let. Me. Go!"

Folding her arms and cocking a prepubescent hip to the side, Covie watched him, lips pursed and head shaking slowly from one side to the other. She waited out his tantrum in silence. Not that she blamed him for being freaked out, but enough was enough already. She'd already told him what needed to happen so she could unwrap the tape from his chest and limbs.

Oliver's struggling slowed to an outraged twitch every few seconds as his breath came in rapid gasps. At last, his frail body gave in and he relaxed his arms and legs, his head lolling back against the chair. He glared at Covie, chest heaving against the duct tape that had kept him safely in the wheelchair while he was incapacitated.

"Are you finished?" she asked.

The boy nodded, sweat dripping from his tangled mess of hair.

"Okay, then." Covie started with his arms and continued on to his legs and finally his chest, rolling the tape up into a ball she threw at the garage door.

"Can I have some water? Please?" Oliver, still breathing hard, rubbed at his arms where the tape had been.

"How about some Pedialyte?" Not waiting for an answer, she reached into her car and grabbed the bottle she'd taken a couple of swallows from last night. She looked at the boy's dry lips and the white crust in the corners of his mouth. "Hold on a sec."

Covie sat the bottle on top of her car and hurried over to a water cooler. The jug on top was empty but the cup dispenser wasn't. She grabbed a cup and returned to Oliver. After filling it halfway, she handed it to him. His hand shook, but he managed to get it to his lips without splashing out too much of the liquid. He emptied it and handed it back to her.

"Would you like some more?" she asked.

"Maybe a little," he said, then asked, "What happened to you?" He pointed at her duct-taped cheek, then looked down at the makeshift dressing wrapped around his naked torso. "And what happened to me?"

She poured more Pedialyte into the cup and put it in his outstretched hand, shaking her head. Covie told him about the deserted hospital, the big plush bear he'd been attached to, and how she'd escaped with him in tow. "Other than that, I don't know. I was hoping *you* could tell *me* the rest of the story."

Oliver handed the paper cup back to her and held up a hand with a shake of his head when she tipped the bottle of liquid toward him with a cocked eyebrow. "That's . . . just crazy," he said. "How old are you? I mean . . . you drove this car?"

"I guess we did kind of skip over the introductions. My name is Covie." It only took her a split second to decide not to tell him the whole truth just yet. "I'm eleven years old. And yeah, I drove this car."

"That's bad-A." He grinned. The film on his teeth made her add "toothbrush" to her mental list of items they needed.

"How old are you?"

He puffed up his skinny chest. "Twelve." He frowned. "I think."

Sadness crept into her heart. *This poor boy has probably been comatose for years.* Anger replaced the wave of sadness as she redoubled her oath to end the plush-demic. She shook her head. A quick change of subject was needed. "What's the last thing you remember?"

"The last thing I remember . . ." His eyebrows scrunched together in concentration. "It won't make any sense unless I start at the beginning." He shifted in the chair, a grimace twisting his face. "But first I need to pee and see why my tailbone hurts."

"Can you stand? Or walk?"

He shrugged. "I guess we're about to find out." He

scooted out of the wheelchair and stood on shaky legs, clutching the armrests for support.

Covie rushed to his side and steadied him, holding on to his arm. "Let me help you."

"Fine. But you ain't goin' into the bathroom with me," he grumbled.

She stifled a laugh. "Eww! Of course not," she said, playing the part of an eleven-year-old girl.

They slowly shuffled to the bathroom, and Oliver shook her hand off his arm when they reached it. He stepped inside and started to shut the door, pausing to stick his head out and say, "And don't stand so close. I don't want you to hear me peeing."

With an eye roll, she stepped away from the door.

Several minutes later, just when Covie was ready to knock and ask if he was okay, the door opened and Oliver hobbled out—a little paler than when he'd gone in. She helped him back to the wheelchair, but he didn't sit right away. Instead, he stared at the worn, cracked faux leather with a puckered brow. "You got a pillow or somethin' I can use? I got a big ol' sore on my crack bone, right at the top."

A bedsore, she guessed, anger welling up again at the treatment this kid had endured. "Yeah. Hold on."

The cushion Covie used to see over the steering wheel fit perfectly in the wheelchair. After getting settled, Oliver turned to her. "It all started with the meteor strike."

CHAPTER
THIRTY-FIVE

"Meteor strike?" Covie repeated. She dragged a folding chair over and sat facing him.

Oliver's eyes glowed with a spark of mischief, a glimpse of the boy he'd been before the evil plush got their hands on him. He nodded with enthusiasm. "Yeah. My buddies and me were having a sleepover outside on Tim's trampoline and we watched it fall from the sky and land in a field. We grabbed our bikes and flashlights and rode out there. It was farther than it looked—it took almost an hour."

"Did your moms know you went?" She couldn't keep the mom-voice admonishment out of her tone. "How many friends were with you?"

He scowled. "Of course they didn't know. No way they woulda let us take off in the dark."

"So what did you find?"

"I was getting to that. Why do girls always interrupt, then get annoyed about not hearin' the whole story?"

"Sorry," Covie said. "But asking questions is a good way to let others know you're listening to what they're saying."

His scowl deepened, but a smile twitched at his lips

beneath it. "What, did your grandma tell you that bit of olden-time BS?"

Laughing, Covie mimed zipping her mouth shut and gestured for him to continue.

"Anyway, as we got closer to the impact zone—that's what it's called when something from space hits Earth," he explained.

Mansplained.

Boysplained.

Covie hid another laugh by coughing into her shoulder.

"It got really foggy, so we ditched the bikes—and to answer your earlier question, there were two friends with me. We ditched the bikes . . ."

He made more detours when telling a story than Emily did, and Covie had thought no one could beat her daughter at making a short story long like that.

"The *experts* figure the fog was actually meteor dust, and me and the guys ingested some of it or breathed it in, maybe, because we got real sick after and had to go to the hospital." The corners of his mouth turned down and he crossed his arms, holding on to his shoulders with his hands. "Tim and Andy got to go home, though."

"And you didn't." Covie wanted to hug him, seeing the sadness in his slumped posture. "Why is that?"

"I don't know." The enthusiasm with which he'd started the story disappeared, and he spoke with a low monotone voice, eyes staring blankly at the floor. "But I wish I would have."

After several minutes of silence, Covie urged him to continue. "What happened at the hospital, Oliver?"

He sniffed and wiped his nose with the back of his hand, then dropped both hands to his lap, fidgeting with his fingers. "They ran all kinds of tests. They took my blood so many times, my arms looked like pincushions. X-rays, CAT scans—they even shoved a huge needle in my hip to get the stuff out of the middle of my bone."

"Bone marrow," Covie said.

"Yeah. Bone marrow. They made me pee and poop in containers so they could test that too." He shuddered. "I just remembered . . . they took something out of my back, too, like some sort of liquid. From my spine."

Spinal fluid, Covie thought. This poor kid.

"I couldn't see *that* needle, of course, cuz it was in my back, and they made me scrunch up into a little ball while they did it. But I bet it was huge too. It felt big."

Where were his parents during all this medical torture? Covie would ask later if he didn't mention it. She didn't want to interrupt him now.

He wiped his fist across his nose again and looked up at her. "I'm cold. You got an extra shirt or something?"

"I don't . . . but . . ." She looked around the garage, her gaze landing on a row of lockers against a wall. "Hang on."

"I ain't going nowhere."

Covie opened each of the four lockers, pleased to see at least one set of dirty coveralls in three of them. Finding the smallest size, she brought them back to Oliver and helped him stand again to put them on. They drowned him, but after she rolled up the legs and sleeves, they didn't look too bad. "Is that better?"

"Yeah. Thanks." He settled back onto the cushion in the wheelchair. "Where was I?"

"The hospital running tests," she reminded him.

His eyes turned cold and his lips flattened out. "Hmph," he grunted. "That got lots worse when the military got involved."

"That explains why I found you in an old military

hospital." Covie had so many questions. "Why *did* they get involved? What did they do to you? I mean, what could be worse than bone marrow samples and spinal taps?" She clamped her mouth shut as she remembered the umbilical cord. That was worse. Way worse.

A scornful laugh, sounding like it came from someone much older than twelve years, tore from his throat. "Oh, you have no idea. Once they found out I had alien DNA in me, they took me to their hospital and wouldn't let me go."

CHAPTER
THIRTY-SIX

With a sharp inhale, Covie jumped to her feet, his words sending a spike of adrenaline into her veins. "*Alien*? As in, from outer space? Extra-terrestrial?"

"Yep." Oliver nodded. "They figured it happened when I breathed in that meteor-dust fog stuff. And I musta breathed in more than my friends, because they didn't have any in their blood."

"Holy crap." She forced herself to sit back down on the edge of the metal chair and leaned forward. "Were you still sick?"

"No! That was the worst thing about it. I felt fine, but they wouldn't let me go home."

Covie crossed her arms and sat back, anger filling her insides. "Tell me everything."

She sat in silence, except for an occasional gasp, while he continued.

Oliver couldn't remember who had given him the plush monkey that was his only toy while confined to the hospital bed, suffering through more tests, always with an IV stuck in one arm or the other. At first, he was kind of annoyed someone would give a stuffed animal to an eleven-year-old, but once the loneliness set in, the monkey became his best friend.

That was before the plushdemic started. Back when stuffed animals were just unanimated toys. Either the nurses took pity on him or got tired of trying to entertain the rambunctious young boy while taking care of their other patients, but they ended up giving him a bunch of medical supplies to play with. Told him to pretend like he was the monkey's doctor.

Among the test tubes, bandage material, tape, gloves, masks, syringes, and other items, his favorite thing was the IV tubing with a fake IV needle—made with a paper-clip—attached to the end. Oliver would jab the paperclip into the monkey's arm and pretend to give it medication through the tubing.

One day, when they had him hooked up to a bunch of monitors with wires on his chest, legs, and head, he dropped the fake IV on the floor. He couldn't reach it from the high bed, especially with the protective side-rails up—and they'd taken the nurse call button away from him days before because of what the nurses called an "abuse of a privilege" and something about "crying wolf" too many times. After waiting for a nurse to come in for what seemed like hours to a bored kid, he gave up on retrieving the fake IV and got the grand idea to pull his IV out of his arm and use that.

So he pulled the tape off, just like he'd watched the nurses do dozens of times, held a piece of gauze from his play supplies to the site, and pulled the IV catheter out of his arm. He taped the gauze down, then grabbed his plush monkey. He'd poked the paperclip into the toy monkey's arm so many times, it was easy to push the real IV catheter through the fake hair and into the stuffing. He wrapped enough tape around it and the plush's arm to secure a jet to a runway—his words—then connected an air-filled syringe to the hub and pushed the plunger like he'd done multiple times a day since he'd been given the "toys."

At this point in Oliver's account, Covie slapped a hand over her mouth, ideas and theories tumbling through her head.

"What?" he asked.

She laid her hand back in her lap and shook her head. "Nothing. What happened then?"

"Well, I got in trouble for taking my IV out and had to get a new one put in. Then they took the monkey and put it on a chair across the room, told me it was bedtime, and turned out the lights." He looked up at her, eyes going wide. "When I woke up in the morning, the dang thing was sitting on my chest. *Smiling* at me."

Patient Zero.

Now it was starting to make sense.

"That means the bear plush I killed wasn't Plush Zero," Covie murmured.

"Huh?"

"Nothing." She tapped her fingers on the metal chair. "What about the big bear plush that was in your room at the hospital?"

"Relax, I'll get to that." He licked his dry lips. "Can I have another drink first?"

She refrained from asking him "What's the magic word?"—such a mom thing to say—and poured more of the drink into his cup and handed it to him.

After swallowing it down, he smacked his lips. "Thanks."

"You're welcome. Now, what happened after your monkey plush became animated?"

Oliver wrinkled his brow. "Animated? Like a cartoon? Huh?"

Huffing out a breath of air, Covie rephrased her question. "What happened after it came alive?"

"Oh. Well, we played." He shrugged. "It was awesome . . . at first. It would play dead whenever someone came in the room. It kept getting smarter and smarter, like it started talking to me a couple of days after it came alive, just a word or two at first, but after about a week or so it could talk in full sentences. We'd stay up super late talking almost every night—the night shift didn't check on me much."

"What did you think? I mean, wasn't it kind of weird?"

"Psh. Yeah, at first. I was super lonely and bored, though, so having a friend was awesome. The monkey started to leave the room at night and bring back extra snacks and drinks for me. He even brought me soda! With caffeine in it!"

"That—" Covie stopped herself from finishing the sentence she always said to Emily when she wanted caffeinated beverages, *That'll stunt your growth*, and changed it to, "That's amazing."

"Yeah." Oliver sighed. "It was. For a while." His enthusiastic demeanor flipped upside-down, the glint in his eyes dulled, and his voice wavered. "Then the nurses stopped coming in to check on me."

CHAPTER THIRTY-SEVEN

Wincing, because she thought she knew what it meant that the nurses stopped coming in, Covie asked something she'd been wondering this whole time. "What about your parents? Didn't they come see you?"

Oliver crumpled inward, hanging his head. "Just my mom. Not very often though."

"And . . . what about after the nurses disappeared?"

"Yeah." He sniffed, still looking down. "Even then. I thought it was weird, especially after the monkey told me what happened to the nurses."

"Which was . . . ?" Even though she knew, she needed to hear him say it.

"He killed them," Oliver whispered.

"But didn't your mom see the plush? Or notice that there was no staff there?" Covie's mind raced, trying to make sense of things. What mother would just let her child suffer like that?

He shrugged. "She acted like everything was normal, and the monkey told me not to tell her anything."

Covie puffed her cheeks and blew air through her pursed lips. Unbelievable. "So what happened then?" He still hadn't told her anything about the big bear plush she'd killed.

"One day the monkey brought other living plush to my room." Oliver raised his head and straightened up a little now that he wasn't talking about his mom. "He'd infected them. That big teddy bear was one of them. A llama, a Pegasus, and . . . I think one more, maybe a seal? And I was like, 'Where did they come from?'"

Plush Zero, the monkey, told him it'd found some friends in the hospital gift shop and they were all going to hang out with Oliver. "It wasn't fun anymore," he said with a quick shake of his head. "The monkey started being mean, and the new stuffed animals acted like his thugs."

Looking down, Oliver gestured to his abdomen, now concealed by the coveralls. "They hooked me up to the bear with that belly-button cord. The bear never left my room—it was both a bodyguard and the main nurse. And I was their hostage."

"This is so crazy," Covie said. The plush she'd come into contact with lately were dim-witted, to say the least. Every single one of them. "How in the world did they know how to do that? The umbilical cord and other medical stuff?"

"The monkey is smart," Oliver said. "It taught itself how to read in, like, a couple of days. It would bring these huge books into my room, said they came from the medical library in the doctors' lounge. It read the instructions out loud while its gang held me down and inserted the cord." His skin blanched and he covered his face for a few seconds.

"Oh, Oliver," Covie whispered, "that must have been awful."

Nodding, he wiped his eyes, then continued, talking

fast like he just needed to get it all out. "They took blood from me once a week. I thought I was gonna die cuz I knew people need blood to live, but I wasn't sure how much of it our bodies make in a week, ya know? So I decided to escape."

He explained how he had climbed to the floor while the bear was asleep—standing at the foot of the bed like a creepy gargoyle—and crawled to the door. His plan had been to go out into the hallway and slam the door on the umbilical cord over and over, hoping to sever it, then find his way to an exit. He was so weak; he hadn't had anything to eat for weeks. The monkey kept telling him he was getting everything he needed from the cord attached to the big bear. He made it out to the hallway, but couldn't shut the door hard enough to do anything to the tether. All that happened was the bear woke up and grabbed him, slamming him back onto the bed.

The second attempt turned out to be even more pitiful than the first. Again when the bear was asleep, Oliver reached into the hard plastic sharps container hanging on the wall next to his bed, squeezing his small hand through the opening, and fished a scalpel out. The llama came in and alerted the bear before he'd even made a scratch in the cord.

They tied him to the bed, just his hands, so he used his teeth to untie himself—it turns out plush paws weren't real great for tying secure knots—then scrambled to the bottom of the bed and wrapped the string around the bear's neck and pulled it tight, using his weight as leverage.

Oliver bared his teeth in an angry grin. "That was the best attempt. That stupid bear thrashed around, trying to get its fat paws between the string and its neck."

His eyebrows came together in a V. "Then it got

smarter and came after me instead of the string. It crushed me so hard against its chest, I thought it was gonna break my back."

Or a rib or two, Covie thought, rubbing her bruised side where the same bear had used the same tactic on her.

"That's when they put me into a coma, I guess." Oliver examined his fingernails. "I don't remember much of anything after that until waking up here."

A sudden thought occurred to Covie. "You said you're twelve . . ."

"Yes. That's right." Oliver's head whipped up and his eyes widened. "If it's still 2032. It is, right?" His voice rose to dolphin levels.

Covie did not want to answer him. But he needed to know the truth, and she was the only one here to tell him. "I'm sorry, Oliver, but it's 2035."

"Wait, so I'm a teenager?" He looked down at his chest, his legs, examined his hands and arms. He unzipped the coveralls and checked his armpits for hair, finding none. "I haven't aged. I'm not getting older. It can't be 2035. It can't . . ." Oliver's breathing sped up. He leaned forward and grabbed Covie's wrist. "How?" he asked hysterically.

Laying a hand on top of his, she spoke with a calm voice. "Oliver, it's okay. We'll figure this out. I promise."

CHAPTER
THIRTY-EIGHT

Food was always a good de-escalator. Covie and Oliver shared a can of mandarin oranges, and he acted like they were the best thing he'd ever eaten. Covie didn't blame him. From what he'd said, he hadn't eaten anything solid for a few years. She hoped it didn't make him sick.

Covie reviewed the pertinent information she'd learned from him. The monkey was Plush Zero. She'd only killed the nurse/bodyguard plush. So where was the real Plush Zero?

"What are you thinking about?" Oliver asked.

Realizing she held the canned fruit halfway to her mouth as she stared into space, she lowered it to her lap. "Do you know where I can find Plush Zero?"

"Plush Zero?" He tipped his head to the side.

"The monkey. It's the first one, the first plush infected with the virus. It's important that I find it."

"I have no idea." Oliver looked at their surroundings, as if realizing where they were for the first time. "Why *are* we hiding out in a garage, by the way? What's going on out there?" He nodded his head toward the door.

Covie sighed. She guessed he wouldn't know about the extent of the plush pandemic. How could he? He'd been locked inside that hospital the whole time. *Literally* the whole time. "What started with your plush monkey toy spread . . . everywhere. Gangs of plush have taken over large parts of the city—large parts of every city. We're right in the middle of one of those areas, and this garage looked like a safe place to rest."

"Is . . . is this all my fault?" He looked even younger than twelve as he gazed at her through thin eyelashes.

"No way. You were just an innocent victim of circumstance."

He shook his head. "How old did you say you are? You sure don't talk like a kid sometimes."

Covie laughed. "You caught me. Can you keep a secret, Oliver?"

He nodded. And she believed him.

She told him what happened to her with the claw machine, that she was really a grown woman trapped inside a little girl's body.

"That's crazy. Totally cray-cray."

Covie frowned. She knew someone who used that ridiculous phrase, and it reminded her of something she hadn't asked him yet. "Oliver . . . the chart on your bed at the hospital said your last name is Connelly. Is that correct?"

"Yes. Why?"

"Well, I have a friend with that last name. At least, I think she's my friend, but right now I'm not so sure."

"What's your friend's first name?"

"Charlotte."

A series of twitches crossed Oliver's face. "That's my mom's name," he murmured.

Is this Charlotte's son?

My Char?

My best friend had a son I didn't know about!

Suspicions turned into awful truths in her mind.

How could Charlotte have let this happen to her son? The Charlotte she knew, the one she'd thought was her best friend, wouldn't have stood by and allowed him to be used as the military's research project, and then, even worse, as an unwilling donor to create an army of unholy plush creatures. The Charlotte she knew didn't even have a son . . . did she?

"Why did you say you aren't sure she's your friend?"

Covie told him about her suspicions: seeing Char with Tom and Emily, Char seeing her through the window and then turning her back on her, letting a plush drive her car from a deserted hospital. "But maybe I'm wrong. Maybe it's all just a bunch of coincidences," she said in response to the crestfallen look on his face.

Getting to his feet faster than she thought he'd be able to, Oliver held to the arm of the wheelchair to steady himself. His face turned red as anger and sadness swept across it. "No. It isn't a coincidence. It's her."

"I'm really sorry, Oliver. I still want to be a hundred percent sure, even though I agree with you. I need to find a computer so I can research the license plate I took a picture of."

He took a few stiff-legged steps over to the car, stretched his back, then walked some more.

"You okay?" Covie asked.

"Yep. Just tired of sitting. That sore on my butt hurts. Do you have any more of the thick bandage stuff you covered my belly button with?"

Covie snickered. "Yeah, but you aren't going to like it."

He scrunched his eyebrows together. "Why not?"

She pulled the box of feminine napkins out of the car and showed it to him. "This was all I could find."

Oliver laughed. "No problem. I used to soak those in

water and throw them at my friends. Or take the paper off the back and stick them to their backpacks."

"Boys," Covie said, rolling her eyes.

"It was hilarious." He reached for the box and pulled one of the bulky pads out before heading to the bathroom at a slow but steady pace.

"Hold on a sec." Covie grabbed the baby wipes and handed them to him. "You should probably clean that wound up a little before putting that pad on it."

"Yes, ma'am." He saluted, then continued his shuffle to the restroom.

Walking a little more comfortably as he returned to where Covie stood near the car, Oliver asked, "Now what?"

"I think I should take you to a real hospital," she said.

"Heck no!" Oliver said. "I'm not going back to a hospital. My mom will just leave me there, or worse, take me back to that old one."

"But you need to get checked out."

"I'm fine. I feel fine. I'm not hurt, just weak. I was on a feedin' tube and unconscious for a while. That's it. Really, I'm fine, just a little weak. Please don't take me back to a hospital."

Tears had lined his lower eyelid. Covie thought to her own experience while doctors were trying to figure out the best diagnosis for her and then subsequent therapy. She knew how Oliver was feeling. All the poking and prodding. It wore on a person. She relented. "Okay, Oliver. But if you take a turn and get worse, promise me you'll let me take you without any complaining.

"Now, we find a computer I can use to verify or disprove that it was your mom's car being driven by a plush at that military hospital. Are you feeling up to a little drive?"

"Let's do this."

CHAPTER THIRTY-NINE

The sun shone in the mid-morning sky, making Covie wish she hadn't lost her sunglasses during her fight with Window and his gang. "Be on the watch out for anywhere that might have a computer we can use."

"Okay?" Oliver squinted, unaccustomed to the brightness of the outdoors. He rolled the window down and took a long, deep breath of the fresh air. "It feels so good to be out in the world again." He turned to her. "What about a library? They have public computers."

"I thought about that, and it's a good idea, but you have to have a library card and permission from a parent to use their computers—and we don't have either." She smirked at him. "Unless you've been hiding a walletful of stuff in those greasy old coveralls."

Oliver rolled his eyes, then sat up straighter and pointed out the window. "How about that hardware store? It looks a lot less run-down than most of these buildings."

The tires squealed just a little as Covie made a sharp turn into the small parking lot of what had been a locally owned hardware store before this area had been taken over by plush. The door hung open a crack, but all the windows were miraculously intact, and the interior lights were on. She parked right in front of the door—there weren't any police cars in this part of town to give her a ticket, so why not?

She looked over at Oliver. "Do you want to come in with me or wait in the car?"

Glancing at the store, then back at Covie, he waffled about it. "I'd like to see what's left in there, but I'm really tired." He raised his bottom off the seat and looked down at the cracked asphalt. "And I don't know if my bare feet can handle that rough terrain. So I guess I'll stay in the car." He slouched down and sighed.

"Okay, I shouldn't be in there long anyway. Roll up your window and lock the doors."

Covie exited the car and grabbed her machete, sliding it into the sheath at her side. A piece of paper taped to the door of the store caught her attention, and she stopped to read it.

The Hapley family would like to thank all of our loyal customers for giving us your business over the last eighty years. We are deeply saddened to leave our store and community in these difficult times. We stayed as long as we could, but this city is in danger. Companies cannot continue doing business in our city's current state. There is no protection from the mobs of plush, no recourse against the animalistic behavior that goes unpunished and unchecked. The danger to our family and staff has grown too severe to remain open, and for that we apologize. We stayed as long as we could. We'll leave the door open in the hope that what's left may help someone in need. Hapley

Hardware will return when this plush pandemic and its aftermath have been dealt with.

With love,
The Hapleys

Anger burned in Covie's chest. That poor family. She pursed her lips as she entered the store, determined more than ever to do whatever she could to put an end to the plush—and that meant finding Plush Zero. Tom had been sure that was the essential piece he and the other scientists needed in order to figure out how to reverse this plush pandemic. His science journal had been clear about that. And she really needed to find that claw machine too. She could do so much more to help if she could be grown-up again.

Right now, Covie didn't know what to do. She was drawn to call Tom, but with her suspicions about Charlotte, she hesitated to reach out. If Charlotte really had abandoned a child, Covie felt dread that she had invited her to take care of her family while she was in this predicament. That fact drove her even harder to find answers. She needed to protect her family.

She'd walked right to the object she needed without even looking as her deep contemplation raged on. A small office in the back of the ransacked store sat virtually untouched. There was an old desk, the top cleaned of everything but an empty wire basket and a computer. Covie flipped the light switch, illuminating the cozy space. Her ire was stoked once more at the thought of this sweet family being displaced by the demented plush.

She sat in the worn leather chair and crossed her fingers as she pushed the power button on the computer. It sprang to life, a lone search-engine icon appearing in the center of the monitor. It appeared as though the Hapleys had erased the hard drive and left this beacon of goodwill for anyone who might wander in and need it. The internet symbol had three full bars.

A miracle!

Having helped a friend track down the name of her cheating husband's mistress a couple of years ago, Covie knew exactly where to go. She pulled up the state DMV site and did a public-record license-plate search using the alphanumerical characters on the plate she'd nabbed a picture of. The resulting information that appeared on the screen didn't give the name of the owner, but there was enough information for Covie to know without a doubt. It *had* been Charlotte's car pulling out of the military hospital parking area—with a plush at the wheel.

The suspicion she'd voiced earlier about her friend turned to worry—and frustration with herself for waiting a full day before investigating it. A plush driving Char's car could mean that Covie wasn't safe. Her heart skipped a couple of beats—it could mean that *Tom and Emily* weren't safe also!

She snatched her phone off the desk and texted her husband: *Hi, babe. How are you and Emily doing? Is everything okay?*

No reply.

She waited several long moments.

Still no answer.

Then her phone rang and Covie jumped. She fumbled with it for a split second until she touched the screen to answer. Tom's caller ID flashed at the top of the screen.

"Hello."

"Who is this?" Tom asked.

Covie forgot about her eleven-year-old voice.

She tried her best to disguise it. Since her transformation, she had only texted Tom.

She cleared her throat. "This is Cove."

"Listen here," Tom said sternly, "I don't know what you did with my wife or if you are working with Plush Zero, but you need to put her on this phone now!"

Covie's heart sank. The fleeting chance that she could rationally talk to Tom about her problem fluttered out the window. She started to cry.

"Tom, it's me," Covie said. No chance her voice was anything other than a young girl's. "Please trust me."

There was a long pause.

"If this is the same little girl who was on my front steps, just know I've called the police and you won't get away with kidnapping my Cove."

All Covie could say was, "I understand."

Tom continued. "And if you're working with Plush Zero, we aren't afraid of you and any plush like you."

The line went dead and Covie sniffed, wiping her nose on her sleeve. She gathered her emotions and realized the only way back to Tom was to find the claw machine. She felt trapped, and the key to this was to get her woman's body back.

What should she do now?

Thinking about Emily being taken by a plush gang reminded Covie that Oliver was alone in the car.

CHAPTER FORTY

Covie rushed through the store, grabbing a pair of rain boots about Oliver's size on her way out, and hurried to the car. Relief washed over her when she saw him in the passenger seat, bobbing his head to the radio.

Covie tapped on the window. Oliver flinched at the sound as his hand flew to his chest. When he saw it was just her, he grinned and shrugged, then reached over to unlock her door.

She slid onto the seat cushion and shut the door, staring out the windshield but seeing nothing as her mind raced. Should she rush home to Tom, to check on him and Emily? Or should she stick to her original plan and go find Plush Zero and the claw machine? Her thoughts went round and round in circles, getting her nowhere. She rested her forehead against the steering wheel.

"What's wrong?" Oliver asked.

Covie had almost forgotten he was there. She sat up, and seeing the rain boots in her lap, handed them to him. "See if those will fit you."

Without taking his eyes off her, he took the boots from

her. "Thank you, but you gonna tell me what's going on? Was it my mom's car?"

Sighing, she nodded. "Yeah. And that makes me really worried about her and my husband and daughter."

"Did you try texting your husband?" Oliver nodded to the phone still gripped in her hand.

"Yep." She checked it again to see if he'd answered. "But he hasn't texted back."

"So . . . what now?" He grunted as he bent over to slide the boots on his feet. "Perfect fit," he said. "Thanks again."

"No problem." Covie turned to him. "I don't know if I should go check on them or stay on course to find Plush Zero and the claw machine. Any suggestions?"

"You said that Plush Zero is the monkey, right?"

She nodded.

"Because he was the first one to be infected?"

"Yes."

His eyes grew round and he looked down at the gauze taped to his arm where the IV had been. "I just remembered something."

"What?" Covie raised her eyebrows.

Oliver's eyes slowly met hers. "Remember how I said they took my blood a lot before they put me in a coma?"

"Yeah, I remember," she said in a hushed tone, anger boiling inside her.

"I remember what they were doing with it." He looked back down at his bandaged arm. "I saw the monkey take blood from me and inject it into a plush—a normal, not-alive plush that started moving right away." He wiped a tear from his cheek with a shaky hand. "That's how he animated the plush, Covie. He used my blood."

"Which is why they kept you there."

"That stupid belly-button cord was like a feeding tube.

The big bear fed me and gave me medication through it to keep me alive and asleep." His voice wavered as he added, "They used me for my blood."

"I wonder how often Plush Zero, or any plush besides the bear, really, went to the hospital?" Covie's mind touched on the hint of a plan.

Oliver rubbed his runny nose across the sleeve of the coveralls. "If they kept the same schedule as before they coma-tized me, it was about once a week. Usually on Thursday or Friday. And the monkey was always there to supervise."

The hint of a plan grew to a fully formed scheme in less than a heartbeat. "Today is Thursday," Covie said, mostly to herself. She focused on Oliver, squinting her eyes as she thought. "What time of day did they do this?"

He shrugged. "I don't know exactly, but I think in the afternoon usually, sometimes later. Sometimes earlier." He tilted his head, rubbing his arm absently. "Why?"

Should she even suggest what she was thinking? This young boy had already been through so much—was it fair to ask more of him? Covie turned away from him, chewing on her bottom lip, face scrunched with indecision.

"Covie," Oliver said, "just tell me what you're thinking already."

She ought to at least give him a chance to agree to her plan. Steeling herself, she looked him straight in the eyes. "I have an idea . . . a way to get Plush Zero—the monkey. But it would mean the two of us going back to that awful hospital room." Covie touched his hand, which peeked out of the too-big coveralls. "I'll tell you the plan, then leave it up to you whether or not we proceed. Okay?"

He nodded, eyes growing wide as he swallowed.

"Okay, so the plan is to go back to the hospital, to your room. You would get in the bed and fake like you're in a coma. I'll wear the big bear's skin and pretend to be the nurse plush with the umbilical cord hooked up—I'll just tape it together where I sliced it. When the monkey comes in, I'll subdue it and find out where the claw machine is. Then . . . I'll gut the unholy creature."

Facing the window on his right, Oliver sat in silence for several minutes, picking at the skin around his fingernails. When he finally turned back to her, his face was set with determination. "Let's do it. Being able to see the stuffing ripped from that nasty monkey is worth the risk." He glanced down at the new rain boots covering his feet. "And I trust you, Covie."

A weight lifted off her chest—quickly replaced with a new one as she remembered that her family might be in trouble.

She started the car.

CHAPTER
FORTY-ONE

"Let's go get this thing over with, then," Covie said.

She drove back to the hospital, parking closer this time, but still hiding the car down a side street. She wrangled the wheelchair out of the trunk—even with shoes on his feet, she didn't think Oliver had enough stamina to walk the half-block to their destination.

They both stayed alert to their surroundings as she pushed him along the cracked, uneven sidewalk, veering off into the road as they neared the parking lot. Covie stopped and readjusted the straps of her backpack, checked that the machete and sheath were still at her side, and confirmed that the Bowie knife was tucked safely in her boot.

There were no cars in the parking lot, at least on this side of the building. Charlotte's car had come from behind the building yesterday, but they'd have to risk it. "You ready?" she asked Oliver.

The boy nodded, looking even paler than usual, his hands gripping the arms of the wheelchair so tight, his knuckles seemed like they would break through his thin skin.

Covie backtracked along the same route she'd used

when leaving yesterday, not wanting to clear another path down the debris-filled hallways. They made it safely inside and back to the dreary room where Oliver had been held captive for so long. Standing just inside the door, Covie surveyed the mess.

"Now what?" he whispered.

"I have to clean this up a bit, then we'll hurry and eat a little something because once I get that stinking pelt on, I won't be able to eat until this job is done." She pushed the remaining bloody stuffing into a pile and wet a dirty sheet to wipe up the blood spatters and goo that had oozed out of the umbilical cord. She moved the IV pole and other equipment back to where it had been before her fight with the bear, using surgical tape to tape broken tubes back together as she went, and rehung the fallen curtain, using tape to secure the torn grommets.

She stood back and surveyed the room, nodding when she decided it was close enough. "I'll be right back," she said to Oliver.

It took her ten minutes to find suture material and another five to find some that was a similar blue to the thread that had been used to sew the bear's mouth shut. She also grabbed a pile of scrubs and as much gauze as her little arms could hold. When she returned, the boy was out of the wheelchair, hobbling down the hall toward her as he held a pair of scissors out in front of him.

The worry lines on his face smoothed as he spotted her. "You were gone a long time."

"Sorry, I had trouble finding what I needed. Are you okay?"

"Yeah. I was comin' to see if you needed help. I was worried a plush got you or something."

She smiled. This young man was brave, and she was

glad he was on her side. "Thank you, Oliver, for having my back."

He shrugged, a bit of color flushing his face and neck. "No biggie."

Back in the room, Oliver watched as Covie sewed the mouth shut on the plush pelt of the bear. After crawling along the floor to find the plastic eye she'd cut out of its face, she popped it back in, taping it from the inside so it would hopefully stay put.

"What're you going to do about all the tears in the . . . skin . . . fur . . . whatever?" Oliver asked.

"I call it a pelt, like from an animal." She held it up to examine the slashes from her knife. "I think I can just tape them closed from the inside, like I did with the eyeball. That surgical tape is pretty strong." After she finished, they shared a can of fruit and finished off the Pedialyte.

Oliver helped her get into the big bear pelt, then made her turn in a slow circle so he could inspect it. "It looks pretty good, except you're too skinny."

Tilting the bear's head down to peer through the thin fabric where some of the fur had been worn off below the eyes, Covie saw what he meant. "Grab all those scrubs, the old sheet, and gauze, and shove it in the pelt with me so I look more . . . *plush*."

Oliver twisted his face in disgust, but he stuffed fistfuls of scrubs, gauze, and an old sheet into the arms and legs of the bear, filling in the too-skinny parts of the disguise. Covie also put her backpack on at the front, plumping out the bear's chest.

"How do I look?" she asked after he rinsed the gore off his hands and arms.

"Better."

"Good. Now take your coveralls off and fold them

up so they'll fit in my backpack, then climb into the bed."
She worked at taping the umbilical cord back together,
then handed the other end to Oliver, now lying in the bed
with a blanket pulled up to his chin. "You can just lie on
that end so it doesn't flop onto the floor."

With one finger and a thumb, Oliver took the cord
from her, grimacing as it touched his skin, and shoved it
under his back. He looked around the room, then down
at himself, before looking back at Covie. "Do you know
how to start an IV?"

She frowned. "I've started a couple on a dummy arm
for work training."

"Well, they're gonna expect me to have one. That's
usually how they get blood out of me."

"Usually?" Covie asked as she looked through a small
supply cart on wheels up by the head of the bed.

"Yeah. If the IV stops working while they're siphon-
ing my blood, they just slice into my wrist." He held up
his arm to show her the scars.

CHAPTER FORTY-TWO

Covie clenched her jaw and muttered, "Evil sons o' bi—"
She spied what she'd been looking for before finishing the expletive.

After a successful IV insertion, they were ready. All they could do now was wait. Covie closed the hospital curtains around her and Oliver as they'd been the day before, then stood guard next to his bed.

"What do we do if it—the monkey—doesn't come?" Oliver asked.

"I've been thinking about that," Covie said, her voice muffled from the plush pelt. "I think that if Plush Zero doesn't show up by tomorrow, I'll get out of this stinking costume and we'll just have to hide somewhere nearby and watch for activity."

As night fell, Oliver slept, and Covie leaned against the bed, her head bobbing with exhaustion.

★ ★ ★

A ray of sun stabbed through a hole in the curtains surrounding the bed, rousing Bear-Covie from a semi-vertical catnap. She straightened and arched her back, wincing behind the bear-pelt face at the many tender muscles in her body. Shuffling over to check on Oliver, she stopped dead and cocked her head toward the room's door.

Muffled voices came from the hallway, getting louder and clearer as they approached. Covie's pulse sped up like she'd just peaked in a cycling class, and she whipped her head toward Oliver, intending to wake him up so he could pretend to be asleep.

His wide eyes told her he was awake and had heard the visitors too. She put a paw to the sewn-shut mouth covering her own as a signal for him to be quiet. He nodded and closed his eyes, lying still.

"I hope the IV ain't workin' today," an annoying, high-pitched voice said. "I like it when I get to slice the little brat's wrist."

A husky laugh was followed by an equally husky voice speaking. "We could always pretend it isn't working. It isn't like the kid's gonna tell on us."

Covie pushed the hospital curtain aside just as the two large plush entered the room, a steel pail in one's hand.

"Heya, Big Bear, what's up?" the giant plush rabbit holding the pail said.

That's the one with the husky voice, Covie thought. It was fortunate that Big Bear's mouth had been sewn shut, because these idiot plush wouldn't expect it to speak. Covie shrugged and turned back to face the bed.

"Uh, Thumper," the big bulldog plush with the high-pitched voice said, "you know Big Bear can't talk, right?"

"Of course I do, doofus. Now get that pail positioned to catch the blood while I check his IV."

Covie tensed, ready to pounce at the two plush before they started the bloodletting. The rabbit lifted Oliver's thin arm, and she took a step toward it.

"You two dimwits haven't even started yet?"

The two stuffies and Covie whirled around at the loud voice. A plush monkey stepped through the door. Plush Zero. The monkey sneered, a large cut above one of its eyes making the sneer look even more menacing. It pointed at the bulldog with a mismatched arm that ended in thick bearlike claws. "Get a move on, Ralph. They're waiting for us at the warehouse. A new shipment came in this morning."

Warehouse? Shipment? Covie didn't want them to take Oliver's blood, but she was even more outnumbered now—and outgunned. The monkey had a knife belt cinched around its blue vest made of plush pelts and a sawed-off shotgun slung on its back. Plus . . . she really needed to find out more about this warehouse. So she continued to play the part of the nurse as the three plush talked.

The bulldog hooked some tubing up to Oliver's IV and let gravity take over as he dropped the open end into the pail, the boy's blood trickling into it. "What we get today oughta be enough for a week or longer, don't ya think, boss?"

Plush Zero scratched at its chipped plastic nose with its normal monkey hand. A spiked ball on the end of its tail dragged on the floor as it moved to observe the progress of the blood collection. "It'll have to be enough. We don't want to overdo it. This kid is the only donor we have."

"Yeah, but there are other ways to make living plush, right?" the rabbit asked. "So we don't really *need* need him." It looked at Oliver with pure malice in its beady eyes.

With a scowl, Plush Zero smacked the rabbit upside the head with its bear-claw hand, causing the big-eared plush to face-plant into the side of Ralph the bulldog.

"Are you questioning me, Thumper? Do you think I'd go to all this trouble if we didn't need the little brat?"

"No, boss." The rabbit plush rubbed its cheek.

"Those other ways make weak plush, like Window. How many times do I have to tell you that we're making an *army* here? We need strength and smarts." Plush Zero nodded toward Oliver. "This kid's blood makes the strongest and smartest. And there is no substitute."

Plush Zero walked along the side of the bed where Covie stood in disguise. The monkey looked like a general inspecting his troops. Stopping, the troublesome plush spun around to face Covie. "Big Bear, change these sheets, they're disgusting."

Covie exhaled slowly, trying to calm her out-of-control heart rate. She moved to the cupboard at the head of the bed, hoping that was where the spare sheets were, careful not to dislodge the taped-together umbilical cord. Hands shaking inside the pelt, she was relieved to see haphazardly folded sheets as she swung the door open.

"Speakin' of Window," Ralph the bulldog said, "did you hear what happened to him?"

Going about the business of changing the sheets, Covie's ears perked up, and she listened with intent to the plushes' conversation.

"Of course I heard, I have ears everywhere. He got taken out by a *little girl*! And our booby-trapped claw machine at Stop a Sec didn't work as planned because of it."

CHAPTER
FORTY-THREE

Covie's muscles jerked involuntarily at the mention of the claw machine. Did Plush Zero know where it had gone? Her plush-covered hands worked reflexively at the job of changing the sheets, rolling Oliver over toward the bulldog and pail to remove the bottom sheet and stuff it under him, then putting the new sheet on and stuffing it under the old one. As she rolled him back toward her, careful not to pull on the IV tubing in his arm, the plush conversation continued.

"Yeah, boss," the rabbit said. "That dumb chicken thought he was gonna take over your spot as leader."

The three plush laughed.

"Too bad there ain't a way we could multiply the brat's blood," the bulldog said in its high-pitched voice. "There's lots of plush toys waitin' at the warehouse to become real boys"—the dog snorted—"you know, like that puppet. Pinochle."

"It ain't Pinochle, idiot," the rabbit said, "it's Pistachio."

These guys are supposed to be the smartest? Covie thought. Maybe they didn't get animated directly by Oliver's blood.

"It's *Pinocchio*, you numbskulls." Plush Zero raised an eyebrow. "When's the last time you two got a booster?"

Booster?

The two underlings looked at each other and shrugged. "It's been a while," Thumper said.

"Well, get on the list. There are over a thousand others waiting for a booster—and it sounds like you two need it."

With a bit of difficulty, Covie shuffled over to the other side of the bed, lifting the umbilical cord over the end so it went with her. She worked around the plush collecting blood as she removed the old sheet and pulled the new one over the mattress, the whole while trying to put two and two together with the plushes' conversation. *Warehouse, booster, army . . .*

"Wait! Stop, nurse!" Plush Zero said. "What is that?"

Fear spiked inside Covie as she whipped her head up to see the monkey staring right at her. *Crap!* Had one of the holes in the bear pelt torn open? Was her cover blown?

The plush boss shook a clawed finger at the bedside table. Covie looked to where he pointed. The empty can of fruit. Her stomach dropped. Why hadn't she gotten rid of that? She turned the bear head back to face Plush Zero, readying for an altercation.

The monkey gestured at Oliver, who continued to play comatose on the bed. "You are only to give him liquids." It pointed to the boy's belly, hidden under the blanket. "No solid foods. Liquids through the umbilical only."

Covie nodded in slow motion.

Plush Zero shook its head, then turned to its minions. "That's enough blood. Let's get going."

The bulldog unhooked the tubing from Oliver's IV and hefted the steel pail, the boy's blood sloshing against the sides. "Help me out here, Thumper. I don't want to spill any."

The three plush left the room, and Plush Zero's voice reached Covie as they walked down the hallway. "Nurse is looking pretty skinny these days. We may need to find a new one."

Covie stood stone still until she was sure the coast was clear. "Oliver, are you okay? We need to follow them."

The boy opened his eyes, the dark circles beneath them even more pronounced in contrast to his ashen skin. "I'm okay, just . . . weak." He strained to sit up, then looked down at the IV in his arm. "Hand me a gauze and some tape, please."

He pulled the IV catheter out and taped the gauze over the site.

Assisting him to stand beside the bed, Covie asked, "Can you help me get out of this stinking pelt?"

Oliver nodded and ripped the pelt open at a spot he knew was held together by tape. She shed the disguise and grabbed the wheelchair, ushering Oliver to sit in it, shoulders slumped and head drooping in exhaustion. She readjusted the backpack straps over her shoulders.

"Hang on." Covie ran, pushing the wheelchair in the direction Plush Zero had gone. At the exit, she stopped and peered outside before proceeding, spotting the three plush piling into a black pickup. She crept out to the parking lot and watched the direction the truck went. Sure they hadn't been seen, she started running again, trying to dodge the big holes in the asphalt for Oliver's sake.

Back at her car, she helped him into the passenger seat, then hurried to the driver's side, leaving the wheelchair at the side of the road. There was no time to wrestle it back into the trunk.

She quickly caught up to the black truck—Plush Zero

drove like an old granny, thankfully. Following at a distance, they turned into an industrial area, where Covie slowed to a crawl while the truck parked in the dirt-covered warehouse yard. Plush Zero, Ralph, and Thumper exited the vehicle and carried the pail of blood into the large metal warehouse.

"What is going on here?" she whispered.

Oliver didn't answer. He stared out at the heavy machinery puffing black smoke out of wide exhausts as the plush inside operated them.

Covie hid her car behind an enormous dump truck listing to the side where a tire was missing. She and Oliver crawled under the out-of-commission dump truck and watched as bulldozers and front-end loaders moved large numbers of unanimated plush into huge mounds. Dump trucks lined up near a crane stationed next to one of the mounds, and the large crane arm picked up a bunch of the stuffed animals, depositing them into the dump truck first in line.

Amidst the roar of the heavy machines, Covie turned her head to look at Oliver. His wide eyes mirrored the confusion and dread clouding her mind. He echoed her question of a few minutes ago. "What is going on here?"

She shook her head disbelievingly. "I don't know. But we need to find out. We need to get inside that warehouse."

Oliver's eyes narrowed with determination. He stared back at the crane as the claw lowered to dish up another load of plush. "Let's do it, then. We just need to get in the back of that dump truck with the stuffed animals." He pointed to well-worn tire tracks leading from the crane around to the back of the warehouse. "That's where they're going."

CHAPTER FORTY-FOUR

In awe of his bravery, Covie followed Oliver as he army-crawled to the side of the dump truck being loaded with plush. They positioned themselves in a spot where neither the crane operator nor any of the truck drivers could see them.

Covie laced her fingers together and gestured for Oliver to put his foot in the stirrup they made, hoisting him up to where he could take hold of the top of the dump bed. In his severe state of weakness, there was no way he'd be able to pull himself up and over, so Covie took hold of the bottoms of his feet and hoisted him up until he tumbled over the side. She climbed in after him, her screaming muscles, bumps, and bruises reminding her of the rough go she'd had over the last few days.

She landed next to Oliver, and they hurried to cover themselves with the unanimated plush as the crane dropped another load on top of them. A grinding of gears was followed by a lurch as the truck moved forward. Covie appreciated the soft cushion of the plush beneath her as the vehicle moved slowly over the rough terrain. The jostling ride went on for about three minutes before the truck slowed further, then made a large, sweeping turn before backing up, the *beep beep* of the backup alert loud even from under a layer of plush animals.

The truck stopped with a rough jerk. Covie looked over at Oliver just as the dump bed started to tilt with a squeal of poorly-greased metal. She latched onto his arm, not wanting to lose him in the mass of stuffed animals. As the bed lifted higher, the plush slid down and out of the open tailgate. Covie and Oliver dug down and pressed their feet against the rough bed to try to keep from sliding along with them, but the angle of the tilt was too much.

"Try to stay covered!" Covie said before they were dumped onto the floor of the warehouse with the other plush. She braced herself for a hard landing, but they fell onto the pile of plush and more of the stuffed animals tumbled out on top of them, mostly covering them. She swore she heard a squeak.

Covie peered out from under the pile. A front-loader tractor chugged forward and scooped up a mound of plush right next to them, dumping it into a big fun-nel-shaped receptacle that dropped the plush, one at a time, onto a conveyor belt.

Still holding Oliver's arm, she rolled, pulling him with her, escaping the pile just before the tractor scooped it up. Covie nodded to a stack of boxes and let go of him to scurry over and hide behind them, the boy following at her heels.

They sat up and leaned against the boxes to catch their breath, Oliver with his eyes closed as his thin chest rose and fell. Covie frowned, worried about his frail appearance.

He opened his eyes, caught her staring at him, and mouthed, "I'm fine." He twisted around, maybe to avoid her concerned gaze, and his eyes widened as he pointed with a shaky hand at a black stenciled label on one of the boxes—"PLUSH SERUM."

After a quick glance to ensure none of the plush workers were nearby, Covie pulled a box to her and opened it. It was full of vials containing a yellow liquid.

Oliver stared into the box, eyes distant, and whispered, "This is all from me."

Covie nodded and shut the box. Where were all these plush coming from? She peered around the boxes. Crates from all over the world were stacked to one side of the large, open space. Plush workers wearing orange vests pried the lids off and emptied the contents into piles for the front-loader to scoop up. Just with her quick glance, Covie saw crates from France, Uganda, and Hong Kong. These weren't the Safe Stuffing plush made by her husband's company, she realized. They were pre-pandemic plush that hadn't yet been animated.

This is a bigger operation than I could have ever guessed, Covie thought.

Someone—lots of someones, from the looks of the operation—was gathering all the plush and shipping them to this location. This warehouse run by Plush Zero.

Mac's earnest proclamation of his mission to rid the world of Safe Stuffing plush before they could be taken and animated came to Covie's mind. It was going to take more than one man to shut this down.

CHAPTER FORTY-FIVE

"I need to see if I can find Plush Zero," Covie whispered. "Do you want to stay here and rest? I promise I won't be gone long."

Oliver shook his head. "No way. I'm going wherever you and your machete go." He paused and took a deep breath.

"True," she said. "You're too important to let them capture you again and bleed you dry."

"I'll do my best to keep up," he said.

Covie nodded. "Stay close to me at all times."

She peeked around the stacked boxes and saw their chance to move. "Follow me." She stood in a crouch so she was still hidden and helped Oliver to his feet. A lumbering bison plush pushed a pallet jack loaded with empty crates toward them. It stared at the floor as it pushed with the crown of its head, a small mouse plush walking in front of the advancing jack to clear a path and direct the bison. "Well, that looks like a good way to get squished," Covie muttered.

When the tall stack of crates drew even with her and Oliver, they stepped from their hiding place and used the moving load as a shield to hide behind. Their progress was slow—thankfully, for Oliver's benefit—as the mouse squeaked at listless, slow-minded plush to get out of the way.

"Move it, ya slugs!" it yelled at some unseen colleagues. Its voice was pitched so high, it hurt Covie's ears.

The procession stopped in a far corner of the warehouse, where the bison dropped the pallet jack's handle with a *thunk* as it hit the concrete floor.

"C'mon," the mouse said over the din of whirring machinery, "the boss wants us to help unload some supplies that just came in."

The plushes' shadows moved toward an open door letting a triangle of sunshine spill across the area. Covie waited until she could detect no more movement near them, then stole a glance around the crates. "Holy sh—" She stopped the curse from escaping as she whipped her head around to look at Oliver, her brows rising to the top of her forehead.

"What?" he whispered.

She shook her head. "You have to see for yourself." She got on her hands and knees and started crawling, stopping to look back and see that Oliver followed her lead. She continued to a pile of unanimated plush just big enough for the two of them to hide behind . . . mostly. She raised up to look over the top of a blue penguin, then gestured for Oliver to join her after making sure it was safe.

Rows of sewing machines lined the area, a plush animal of one kind or another sitting or standing next to each one as they hummed and whirred at a fever pitch. A sparkly green dinosaur plush the size of a miniature pony stalked between the rows, barking out insults to any of the workers it deemed to be going too slow. A billy club hung from a strap on its red vest. It leaned over a threadbare otter with a ping-pong paddle attached where its tail should have been and growled, "Faster, water rat! Your pile hasn't grown since my last lap down this aisle!"

The otter flinched away from the billy club as it swayed above its head. The dinosaur stepped back and nodded as the frenzied otter pushed the furry material faster beneath the rapidly yo-yoing needle.

"And you!" The red-vested dinosaur pointed a clawed finger at a group of plush squirrels. "I know you can stuff faster than that. They don't need to be perfect, they're just going to be soldiers when we bring these bastards to life."

Covie and Oliver ducked down when the dinosaur turned its sparkling head in their direction.

"Homer!" it yelled. "Get over here and start loading these plush into the crates."

"Time for us to move," Covie whispered.

They scooted off, hiding behind rolls of stuffing piled high. She thought out loud while Oliver worked to catch his breath. "Plush Zero isn't just animating the plush from all over the world—he's creating more of his own to animate." She shook her head. "This operation is way bigger than I thought."

"Yeah. We gotta find a way to end this." Oliver's pale skin and sunken eyes didn't diminish the determination in his voice. "Let's go see if we can find that nasty monkey."

"Agreed. Let's start by finding out where that conveyor belt is going."

They snuck to the room where the conveyor belt ended. The plush workers were so intent on their jobs, it was easy for Covie and Oliver to remain unnoticed. A line of worker plush stood next to the conveyor belt, plucking the unanimated plush from it as they moved toward the end. The workers sorted the stuffed toys into bins according to size.

Oliver pulled on Covie's arm. She looked at him, then followed his horrified gaze to the tables set up next to each of the sorting bins. A panda plush with a peg leg made out of a toilet plunger opened a box of serum, plucked a plush from the bin to his side, and injected it before throwing the lifeless toy onto a pile a few feet in front of where Covie and Oliver hid. The pile shifted, and the blood in Covie's veins turned cold as a plush buried beneath its brethren dug a passage through them like a zombie clawing its way out of a grave.

One by one, the injected plush twitched to life and crawled, rolled, or slithered out of the mound, then stumbled around like brainless living dead.

CHAPTER FORTY-SIX

A stuffed clown raven, the sight of which sent Covie's heart rate into orbit with irrational fear, wobbled into the large room, the orange yarn-hair on its head waving as the top half of its body swayed in uncoordinated motion with each ungainly step. It pushed a pair of oversized glasses up the bridge of its nose with one hand, holding a clipboard with the other. Coming to a stop amidst the wandering, newly animated plush, it pulled a pen from a pocket of its red vest, moving a badge of some sort out of the way to reach it.

The clown pointed in turn at five of the stumbling plush, made a note on the clipboard, and in a rumbling voice more akin to an avalanche of boulders, ordered the plush to follow it. The smile painted on the clown's face elicited no joy, only creepy serial killer vibes. It led the quintet into an adjoining room and shut the door.

Covie released her held breath and shuddered. She *hated* clowns. From Ronald McDonald to Pennywise—it didn't matter, they were all extremely disturbing.

She turned to Oliver, and his large tear-filled eyes caused her to forget about her clown phobia. "Let's get out of here," she whispered.

They made their way back out to the parking lot without being seen. The big black pickup truck Plush Zero and his bloodletting minions had arrived in was no longer parked where it had been. Covie and Oliver rushed from one hiding spot to another until they reached the broken-down dump truck she'd left her car behind.

Secured inside the locked car, Covie looked at Oliver as he leaned his head back on the seat, eyes closed.

"This is . . . just . . . crazy," she said.

"Yep." Oliver's eyes remained closed.

"I mean . . . I had no idea the plush had the mental capacity to pull an operation like this off. Most of them are just so dumb."

Her mind darted from one thought to the next as she listened to the heavy breathing coming from Oliver in the seat next to her. She needed to alert someone. But who? She'd already experienced the police not taking her seriously in her current prepubescent state. And where had Plush Zero gone? They'd seen him enter the warehouse, but there was no sign of him now. There had to be more areas of the warehouse they hadn't seen. Where had Ralph and Thumper taken the pail of Oliver's blood?

"This is my fault." Oliver's shaky voice interrupted her thoughts. "I'm their creator. If it weren't for me, this would never exist."

Covie laid a hand on his arm. "No, Oliver, this is *not* your fault. You have had no say in any of this. No one asked for your consent. You had no way to know what your blood would do to the stuffed monkey—no one could have guessed what would happen." She squeezed his arm gently. "They put you in a *coma* and stole your blood!"

A tear trailed down his cheek as he stared at the dashboard. "But it's *my* blood that's bringing them to life. *I* am Patient Zero! Plush Zero is my blood relative." He finally turned his head to look at her, and his eyes narrowed in a look of determination and anger. "But I'm no longer their victim. They will never get another drop of blood from me." He swiped the moisture from his face and asked, "How are we going to stop them?"

"I don't know. This is so much bigger than I'd ever imagined. The claw machines are just a small part of the whole operation." She shook her head. "I can't believe they're actually sewing their own army."

"You said your husband is working on a cure, but he needs Plush Zero's blood to do it. So we need to find that scumbag monkey again."

Covie nodded slowly, her thoughts churning, trying to piece together something nagging at her brain. "Yes. He needs Plush Zero's blood because it was the first infected plush and he thinks they can reverse engineer it to find an antidote." She grinned as a brilliant idea formulated. "But we have something even better, don't we?"

Oliver scrunched his brow. "We do?"

"You said it yourself a minute ago. You are *Patient* Zero. The scientists don't know about you; they don't know there *is* a Patient Zero they should have been looking for."

He perked up. "Do you think they can use *my* blood to find a cure?"

"I'm almost sure of it."

"Well, what are we waiting for? Let's go see your husband! Plus, I want to go home."

Covie frowned. She saw a flashback of Charlotte standing in her home, laughing with Tom, her arm around Emily . . . the look her "friend" had given her when she'd seen her peeking in the window. Charlotte's car leaving the deserted hospital, driven by a plush. Leaving Oliver in the hands of the military and then the sadistic Plush Zero. Could she trust Charlotte? And since Charlotte had been with Tom—could she trust her husband? A pang of guilt swept through her at that thought. He'd never given her a reason not to trust him. But . . .

"What? Why are you frowning?" Oliver asked.

"I'm just . . . I'm not sure Tom is the right person to go to with this."

"Why not?"

Yeah, why not? Covie rubbed her suddenly unsettled stomach. She couldn't risk it. She couldn't risk Oliver becoming imprisoned by the plush again. She really wanted to trust her husband—*should* trust him—but she couldn't take that chance if even a miniscule doubt remained. She didn't want to voice her misgivings out loud. "He doesn't know about the body-switch thing. And he thinks I'm either kidnapped or in quarantine at the hospital."

"For what?"

"I told him I was having some bad side effects from a medication I'm—" She drew in a quick breath and smiled as an idea struck. "I know who we can go to about this."

CHAPTER FORTY-SEVEN

Covie fished her phone out of her pocket and hit the button to bring it to life. But nothing happened. The screen remained dark. After a moment of panic, she realized she hadn't actually charged it in far too long. She grabbed the phone cord plugged into her car and shoved it into the end of her phone. Knowing it would take a few minutes to turn on, she started the car and pulled away from the warehouse of horrors.

"Well," Oliver said, hands held out in exasperation, "are you going to tell me who we're offering my blood to?"

"Oh yeah. Sorry. Her name is Dr. Mary. She works for SynthNA and oversees my Plathos Disease treatment and manages my Phyzcoxin dosage."

"P-Plathos Disease? What's that?"

Of course Oliver wouldn't know what that was. Even if it was something he would have paid attention to at his age, he'd been stuck in that dreadful hospital while the whole thing was rolling out. "It's a fairly new disease that causes your DNA to unravel. I've had to have injections of a medication called Phyzcoxin in order to stay in one piece."

"Oh. That sounds . . . bad."

Covie pulled over to the side of the road. "It would be terrible without the treatment. Deadly."

"Maybe that has something to do with your"—he waved his hands up and down to indicate her body—"childish predicament."

She snorted. "Could be. Maybe you should be a scientist when you grow up."

Oliver shrugged. "Yeah. Maybe."

The phone turned on, and after waiting for it to cycle through its process, she noticed her location pin didn't go through. But no matter—she knew right where to find ground zero of the plush. She called Dr. Mary from her contacts. Because of the short amount of time Phyzcoxin spent in trials, the doctor had given her personal cell number to all of her Plathos patients in case they developed new side effects or worsening symptoms.

"Hello, Covie," Dr. Mary answered. "How can I help you?"

"Hi, Dr. Mary." Covie deepened her voice as well as she could to sound more grown up. "Are you in the office today?"

"I'm at the lab today."

"Mind if I stop by? I'm having some weird side effects since my last injection." She decided it was better to ask for the doctor's help in person—so she couldn't hang up when she heard the unbelievable story.

"Sure. I'll be here for another couple of hours."

"Great." Covie briefly closed her eyes in relief. "I'll be there soon."

As they headed back into the city, the car "dinged" and the fuel light came on. "Crap," she said. "I'm going to have to stop at an abandoned gas station before we reach the city. I can't let people see me driving or pumping gas."

She pulled into a gas station where the attached convenience store lay in shambles, but at least two of the gas pumps appeared to be working. Covie surveyed their surroundings before exiting the car. "You stay right there." She couldn't help but think of Emily sitting right where Oliver sat the day this whole body-swap thing had started.

"Where else would I go?" He rolled his eyes.

Covie smiled at the familiar preteen gesture. As she pumped the gas, she thought about her daughter. She needed to get back to her somehow. Even though she'd only been away for less than a week, it seemed like months. She missed Emily. And Tom. And her normal life.

"Covie!" Oliver's alarmed yell brought her out of her reverie.

Senses on high alert, her eyes darted around as she reached for her machete—which she'd left in the car. Oliver pointed behind her, and she whirled around, pulling the gas nozzle from the tank. It had worked once as a weapon, it would work again. She held it in front of her in both small hands as a group of at least five plush rushed toward her from the darkened store. No way she'd be able to get back in the car before they reached her. "Oliver!" she yelled. "Stay inside and lock the doors!"

She swung the nozzle at a big-eyed, multicolored puppy plush, knocking it away from her. Its fellow gang members charged around either side of the pump, and Covie lost her grip on the nozzle as a bird plush leapt at her. Grabbing it around the neck, she flung it across the small strip of asphalt. Cursing, she stomped on the head of a pink lizard plush and reached for the Bowie knife in her boot. A kangaroo almost as big as her soared toward her feet-first when she glanced up, still struggling to free the knife. The big plush feet slammed into her chest, knocking her to the ground.

Her injured ribs flared with pain as her back met the asphalt. The plush gang piled on her chest and limbs. Covie thrashed from side to side, plucking the plush animals from on top of her and flinging them as far as she could—which, due to the awkward position she was in, wasn't very far.

The passenger door of the car opened and Covie's heart fell. "Oliver, no! Stay—" The kangaroo plush stuffed its tail in her mouth, gagging off the rest of her warning.

Oliver swung the machete just hard enough to knock the kangaroo off Covie's chest and open a small gash in the plush's shoulder. He kicked two more of the unholy creatures off her, then she rolled over and jumped to her feet.

"Here." Oliver handed the machete to her, then took a karate stance as they faced their attackers.

The kangaroo's head plopped to the ground with the first swing of her machete, splattering blood and stuffing on her boots. Another swipe of the wide blade chopped the lizard in half, the two halves propelled forward by the still-churning legs. Covie stomped on the head and sliced through its neck.

The bird plush tangled its feet in Oliver's hair while it plucked at his head with its substitute beak made out of two broken spoons. Covie grabbed it around the neck, slammed it to the ground, stepped on its body, and pulled, ripping its head off with a spray of bloody stuffing.

A sharp pain to her right forearm almost caused her to lose her grip on the machete. She sucked in a breath and reached for the mangy ferret plush whose needlelike teeth bit into her flesh. Before the fingers of her left hand even brushed its fake fur, the plush disintegrated into a puff of colorful ash.

CHAPTER
FORTY-EIGHT

"What the . . ." Covie watched the multicolored ash float to the ground.

The remaining two plush skidded to a stop at her feet, looked at the ashy remains of their comrade, turned, and bolted with screeches of terror.

"How did you do that?" Oliver asked.

"I . . . I don't know." Covie blinked, staring as the last of the ash settled next to her feet. The pain in her arm went from stabbing to a dull throb; small dots of blood oozed from the multiple puncture wounds. "That was . . ." She shook her head. "That was . . . so—"

"Awesome!" Oliver interrupted. "Totally awesome."

She allowed a thin smile to cross her lips. "Yeah. But we should get going." She wiped the machete blade off on the kangaroo's pelt, deciding against taking the time to gut them. With one last glance at the pile of ash, Covie placed the gas nozzle back in the pump, then climbed into the driver's seat of her car.

Covie eyed the secretary through the glass door. "This

might be a little more difficult than we thought." She'd seen this secretary in action before—she was no-nonsense and took no crap from anyone when it came to protecting her doctors and lab techs from unnecessary interruptions. Which was normally a good thing.

"Why? Your doctor knows you're coming, right?" Oliver asked.

"Right. She knows that *grown-up* Covie is coming. But I don't look anything like grown-up Covie."

"Oh. Yeah." He shrugged. "We'll just have to talk our way in there."

"Yep." She took a deep breath, pushed the door open, and stepped up to the front desk.

The secretary took in the children's shabby appearance with narrowed eyes. "Can I help you?"

Covie cleared her throat and smoothed her dirty shirt. "Yes. I need to see Dr. Mary, please. She's expecting me."

The woman raised an eyebrow and pursed her lips. "Where are your parents?"

"Not able to come with us. It's about my mom. It's vital that I speak with her." Covie folded her arms across her chest. "Plus, you know the law. We don't need parents to see doctors anymore."

"The doctor knows we're coming," Oliver added.

The secretary shook her head. "She definitely would have told me if she was expecting a couple of *children* to visit her today." She leaned forward and stared down her nose at them. "And she didn't."

Covie held her injured arm out. "But I have a wound. And I know Dr. Mary. She's my doctor."

"Now I know you're lying because Dr. Mary does *not* see children."

"Can you just call her and tell her that Co—"

"The only call I'm going to make is to the police if you are still standing here in three seconds."

The half-dozen people in the waiting room were no longer staring at their phone screens, but watching the interaction with facial expressions ranging from amusement to concern.

The woman picked up her desk phone and pressed it to her ear.

"Okay." Covie held up a hand in surrender. "We'll leave."

As she and Oliver turned toward the door, she spied Dr. Mary coming around a corner into the waiting room. Covie grabbed Oliver's hand and pulled him along as she rushed to the doctor. Dr. Mary frowned and took a couple of steps back.

Knowing this was her only chance, Covie declared loudly, "My mom, Covie White, is sick from the new SynthNA medicine."

The doctor looked up at the patients staring at them and smoothed her face into a reassuring smile. "I'm sure everything is just fine. No need to worry." She looked back at the two children and said in a quiet voice, "Why don't we go to my office so we can talk."

Covie nodded as the tightness in her chest relaxed.

They followed Dr. Mary down a maze of hallways to her office. The doctor sat behind her desk. "Have a seat. I was expecting your mom. I spoke with her about an hour ago on the phone. What is this all about, and where is she?"

Covie swung her legs back and forth, too short to reach the floor while sitting on the fancy office chair. "Okay, Dr. Mary, this isn't really about my mom." Covie rushed to tell her about Oliver's blood and their theory that it could be used to reverse the plushdemic.

As she spoke, the doctor looked back and forth between them, disbelief showing in her gaze.

"Show her, Oliver." Covie elbowed the boy in the arm. "Show her the scars on your arms and belly."

Oliver pushed his sleeves up to reveal small scars up and down the veins in his arms from needle sticks. He slowly unzipped the front of the coveralls, redness creeping into his cheeks in sharp contrast to his pale skin. He removed the dressing and Dr. Mary gasped.

"Oh, you poor boy." She shook her head. "And how long were you there? In the hospital?"

"A long time." Oliver looked down as he pressed the dressing against his wound again, then zipped the coveralls up. "From before the stuffed animals came alive, till she rescued me a couple of days ago."

The doctor covered her mouth in shock.

"What do you think, Dr. Mary? Do you think Oliver's blood, since he is Patient Zero, can help you find a cure?" Covie leaned forward and laid her arms on the desk.

"Perhaps. I'd like to run some tests on it, if you'll let me."

Since Plathos Disease was discovered, laws were passed so kids could give consent for medical treatment and didn't need parents to sign off on it.

"Yeah. That's why we're here." He didn't say "duh," but Covie could hear it in his voice.

Dr. Mary nodded and started to stand, but sat back down, looking at Covie's arm. "What happened to your arm, young lady?"

"Oh yeah," she said. "I meant to ask if you have a bandage I can use."

"Of course, but . . . that looks like a bite mark. What bit you?" Her brow furrowed.

"A plush. It's been a really long day." Covie sighed.

"A plush?" Dr. Mary lifted her arm and examined the wound. Dried blood indicated where the teeth had punctured the skin, and the surrounding skin was slightly inflamed. "I'd like to run some tests on your blood too. To check for infection."

CHAPTER
FORTY-NINE

The doctor explained that it was unlikely any infection would show up this soon after the bite, but she'd like to take an early sample to compare to subsequent samples as she followed the course of the injury. She'd never known someone who'd been bitten by a plush. Most of the monsters didn't even have teeth. And if they did, they were made out of foam and felt.

After obtaining Covie's and Oliver's verbal consent, Dr. Mary drew small tubes of blood from each of them in her office. Covie got the feeling she wasn't ready to let her coworkers in on the secrets she'd just learned.

"Wait here, I'll be back in about ten minutes." The doctor locked her office door on her way out so no one would walk in on the kids.

Covie leaned her head back on the chair and closed her eyes. Finally, someone who was willing to help her.

"You okay, Covie?" Oliver asked. "How's your arm?"

"It's okay. It stings a little where the doctor scrubbed it, but it feels better to have it covered up with a bandage. This too." She touched her face where the doctor had removed the duct tape, cleaned the wound there, and applied some adhesive strips to keep the cut closed. Then Covie had put another piece of duct tape over the wound. To her, it was a mark of the battle. A symbol of war that she wore proudly. By all means, it was the first cut she'd ever received from a plush before.

"Covie?"

"Hmm?" She kept her eyes closed, on the verge of falling asleep.

"What are we going to do after this? Where . . . where are we going to sleep and stuff? If you know my mom, shouldn't we go see her?"

Oliver was right. But there were so many unknowns that she wanted to focus on the task at hand. She fought the thought that if she didn't take Oliver to his "mom," possibly she was holding a child against his will. What did they call that? Kidnapping? Child endangerment? But her justification was she didn't know if Char was truly evil and didn't want to rock the apple cart with that revelation. She also didn't think she had enough clout to be barking up the police tree by alerting them. Plus, she already tried to get them involved and was welcomed with a big nothing sandwich.

So here she was with Oliver. She would make sure he stayed safe, and once she got her body back and delivered the cure to Tom and the authorities, she could blow the whole lid off of her best friend being involved with Plush Zero. Until then, she needed to lie low.

Covie opened one eye and looked at him as he bit his bottom lip. She wished she could just take him home—her home—and tuck him into a nice warm bed with soft, clean sheets. But that couldn't happen until she got her body back. "I don't know, but don't worry, we'll figure something out."

It ended up taking Dr. Mary over twenty minutes to

return to her office. She was quiet when she entered and as she moved to her desk and sat. She twisted her mouth to the side as she looked at Covie for several seconds without speaking.

"Is something wrong?" Covie asked, resisting the urge to squirm in her seat under the doctor's scrutinizing stare.

Dr. Mary cleared her throat and looked down at her desk, tapping her fingers on the desk calendar there. "So . . ." She met Covie's eyes again. "You're Covie White's daughter? I didn't catch your name."

"Em . . . Emily." Something was up. What could the doctor have seen in Covie's blood to make her look so . . . suspicious?

"Well, Emily. I'm a little bit confused after taking a look at your blood under my microscope."

"Confused? Why?" Covie asked, wary of what the answer would be.

"It appears that you have Plathos Disease like your mom. And on the detached chromosomes in your blood, I saw Phyzcoxin molecules." The doctor raised an eyebrow. "But I never inject kids with Phyzcoxin. It isn't approved for kids."

"Oh." Covie had no idea she'd be able to tell all that from a tiny little blood sample.

"So . . . how did you get those molecules in your blood, Emily?" The tone of Dr. Mary's voice wasn't unkind, but it was demanding of an answer.

Covie glanced over at Oliver, who had sat up straight from the slumped position he'd been in while the doctor was out of the office. He nodded. "Tell her."

"Okay," she said, "this might be hard to believe."

"Try me." Dr. Mary smiled and shook her head. "Living plush roaming the streets is hard to believe.

Unraveling DNA is hard to believe. I doubt what you have to say will be any more surprising than those things."

Covie uttered a short laugh and nodded. "Okay, then. I'm not Covie's daughter. I *am* Covie." She explained about the claw machine and her subsequent transformation into the tween girl before her.

"That is . . . wild." Dr. Mary rubbed her temples. "If I hadn't seen the Phyzcoxin in your blood, I might be more reluctant to believe you. But wow. Covie, that's crazy. I'm sorry this happened to you."

Covie loosened her grip on the arms of the chair. "Thank you."

"Well, the good news is you are showing no signs of infections from that bite," Dr. Mary said. "Did anything weird happen afterward?"

"Actually, yes," Covie responded. "The plush that bit me disintegrated into multicolored ash."

The doctor's eyes widened. "I keep thinking you can't surprise me any more than you already have—and then you do."

"Too bad it didn't happen to all of them," Oliver said.

"Yes," the doctor agreed, narrowing her eyes. "That gives me an idea." She pressed a button on a small black device clipped to her name-badge lanyard. "Carlton."

"Yes, Dr. Mary?" a male voice responded.

"Can you please come to my office?"

"Sure thing. On my way."

Covie tensed. "Who's Carlton? And what's your idea?" She really didn't want word getting out about her condition, but even more important, she didn't want anyone to know who or where Oliver was. If Plush Zero found out . . .

"Carlton is one of my lab techs. My most *trusted*

lab tech," Dr. Mary said. "And I want to run some tests before I tell you my idea, just in case it doesn't work."

Before Covie could protest, a twenty-something man stepped into the office and walked to Dr. Mary's desk. He glanced at the two children and tipped his head, looking a bit confused to see them there. "What can I do for you, Doctor?"

"I need you to go out on the street and find a plush for me." She said this as if it were a daily request, expected almost. "Bring it to the basement lab."

Without blinking an eye, Carlton the lab tech said, "Will do. Be right back."

Dr. Mary stood, donned her white lab coat, and motioned for Covie and Oliver to follow her. As they rode the elevator down to the basement, she asked Covie if it was okay to draw some more blood from her.

"Yeah, sure," she consented. The doctor seemed to be trying to hold back her excitement, but it seeped through. And it was contagious. Covie couldn't wait to see what the genius doctor had planned.

CHAPTER FIFTY

The elevator doors opened on a moderately sized lab with bright lights and shiny surfaces covered with instruments and machines. The odor of chemicals reminded Covie of her husband's lab at the toy company.

"Don't touch anything, please," Dr. Mary said. "You can sit over there." She pointed to a corner desk where a couple of folding chairs stood.

"Dr. Mary." Covie put a hand on her hip. "I know I look like I'm eleven, but inside, I'm still an adult."

The doctor barked a short laugh. "Don't worry, Covie, I would have said the same to you in your adult form or anyone else who stepped off that elevator—regardless of age."

Covie relaxed her annoyed stance. "Okay, then."

"I'll gather the stuff to draw your blood again," Dr. Mary said. "I'd like to take more this time—several tubes, if that's okay."

***

As the doctor wrapped the stretchy bandage around Covie's arm where she'd drawn the blood, the elevator opened. Carlton stepped out holding a wriggling duffle bag. "Where should I put this?" he asked.

"One of the exam tables, please," Dr. Mary said.

The lab tech took the bag over to a corner with two curtained-off gurneys and deposited it on one of them.

Covie stood so she could see what the doctor was doing at a lab table a few feet away. Dr. Mary used a syringe to extract a small amount of her blood from one of the tubes. She looked over her shoulder at Covie and Oliver. "You can come watch if you want."

Of course they wanted! They followed right behind Dr. Mary as her heels clicked on the tile floor. "Okay, Carlton, take it out of the bag, but make sure you have a secure grip."

The lab tech nodded and unzipped the duffle. He gripped the furry little llama around the neck as he lifted it out. It struggled and whined, trying to get free. It was one of those cute plush with the big eyes that looked so sweet and innocent. Covie almost felt sorry for it as it kicked its legs in desperation.

Its cuteness did not affect Dr. Mary, however, as she pinned it against the exam table and injected it with Covie's blood. Before she fully withdrew the needle, the plush disintegrated into a pile of colorful ash.

The doctor smiled wide as she engaged the protective shield over the needle, then dropped it in a red sharps container. "Do you know what this means?" Her voice practically trembled with excitement.

Oliver and the tech shook their heads.

"My blood destroys plush?" Covie responded.

Eyes sparkling, Dr. Mary said, "Something within your blood, Covie. I believe it's the Phyzcoxin in your blood that causes this immediate and catastrophic reaction in the plush. I'll need to run more tests . . . but this is it! This is how we end the plush pandemic!"

Covie looked at Oliver. "That means we don't need your blood to find a cure. Maybe you can keep it for yourself for once."

His eyes glistened and the tenseness in his shoulders relaxed. "Good."

Dr. Mary put a hand on his back. "I mean, your blood is cool and all, what with the alien DNA, but it doesn't kill the plush. There's—"

"Alien DNA?" Carlton's eyebrows shot up to his hairline.

"Yes," the doctor said. "I'll explain it all later. But as I was about to say, there's no need to take the time to retrofit a cure out of your infected blood now, Oliver. SynthNA has a whole building full of Phyzcoxin that will do the job!"

Covie thought about Plush Zero's operation going on at the warehouse. More and more plush were being animated by the second as they stood there around an ash-stained sheet. "This is fantastic, but what now? What's the plan?"

"I need to contact the President of the United States. We'll need the government's authorization and help to disseminate the serum." Dr. Mary paced and mumbled as she typed notes into her phone. "They'll need to mobilize the National Guard."

"That'll take too long." Covie knew that once the government was involved, they'd have to fight their way through a bunch of red tape before any action was taken. "We need to act now."

Oliver folded his skinny arms and nodded. "I'm with you, Covie. Do you have a plan?"

A slight smile touched her lips at the conviction in his voice. "First, we need to find Mac."

"The weird dude with the metal mask you told me about?"

"Yep."

"Wait." Dr. Mary stopped pacing and looked back and forth between them. "You can't leave. I still need to run more tests."

Anger prickled at Covie's spine, and she resisted the urge to ram her shoulder into the doctor's gut and escape from the basement lab. She drew in a breath. *Reason first, violence if that doesn't work.* "Dr. Mary, there's a whole warehouse full of plush that need to be stopped immediately, not after Congress spends weeks fighting over what should be done and how we should do it and who should get the credit. Let us go get the annihilation of this plague started while you jump through the hoops to get the government involved. You have my phone number. I promise I'll come back if you need more of my blood or anything."

"But . . . you're just children."

"I'm not a child." Covie clenched her teeth in exasperation. "And we'll have help."

"Right, sorry." The doctor rubbed her temples. "I keep forgetting. Okay. Carlton will walk you out. I'll call if I need you."

They followed the lab tech to the elevator and he swiped his badge to call it down from above. The light over the door lit up with a *ding*.

"Wait." Covie rushed over to the doctor. "Can I have some of those vials of my blood?"

Dr. Mary pulled four of the tubes out of the pocket of her lab coat and handed them to her. "Good luck."

Covie nodded, gripping the tubes as she hurried back to the elevator, where Carlton now held the door open, waiting for her.

CHAPTER FIFTY-ONE

It would be dark soon. The sun slid down the western sky in colorful slow motion as Covie and Oliver buckled themselves into her car. Their eyes met over the console and their faces cracked into twin grins.

"You ready?" Covie asked him.

He nodded. His stomach growled, and he looked down at it, then back up at her. "Maybe we should eat something first."

Covie laughed. "Good idea." She reached into the back seat, grabbed her backpack, and handed it to him. "Get us both something out of here while I call Mac."

As Oliver dug through the bag, she dialed Mac. He answered on the third ring. "Covie. What's up?"

"Do you know the big warehouse over in the old industrial park by the train tracks?"

"Yeaahh."

"Meet me on the west side, on the outskirts so we're hidden from view."

"Umm, okay. Why?" he asked.

"I'll explain when you get there, but believe me, you're gonna want to be there."

Mac growled. "Okay, kid, but this better be good."

"It is. See you in fifteen minutes." Covie ended the call and dropped her phone into the cup holder.

"Here." Oliver handed her a can of fruit and a mangled granola bar, then fished two bottles of water out of the pack.

* * *

Covie parked the car behind a thick cement wall outside the warehouse yard and waited for Mac.

"You sure you can trust this guy?" Oliver asked.

"As sure as one can be after only knowing someone for a very short time." She nudged him with her elbow.

"Ha. Right. Like me an' you." He grinned, then fell silent as he stared out the window.

"Exactly. And he is determined to rid the world of plush. Just like us."

"So what's the plan?" Oliver turned toward her.

"Let's wait until Mac gets here so I only have to go over it once," Covie said.

He nodded. "'Kay. I'm gonna wait outside. My butt hurts from sitting."

She'd forgotten about his bedsore. He had to be miserable, yet he'd hardly complained at all. Tough kid. "Good idea. I'll join you."

They didn't have to wait long. The deep rumble of Mac's truck reached them before it turned the corner to where they could see it. Wearing the metal plague mask, he opened the truck's rust-pocked blue door, obviously not the original since the rest of the dented behemoth was red. Two cobra decals reflected off the hood. He got out, his plush-pelt coat swaying with the movement, and slammed the door, which protested with a screech, then stepped over to Covie and Oliver.

He looked Oliver over with his exposed eye. "I see you found a friend."

"This is Oliver."

"Hey, Oliver. I'm Mac." He glanced at her car. "Don't tell me you drove this car by yourself."

Covie shrugged.

Mac put his hands on his hips and looked up at the moon. "I guess I shouldn't be surprised." He turned his gaze back on her with a sigh. "So, what's this all about?"

Covie gave him a quick rundown of what her Phyzcoxin-containing blood did to plush that came in contact with it.

"Awesome!" Mac jerked his head toward the building. "What's with the warehouse?"

"There are about a million plush in there," Oliver blurted. "Animated ones and about-to-be-animated ones."

Mac's ice-blue eye narrowed in anger. "Explain," he said to Covie.

The sky darkened as she told him about Plush Zero's complex operation to infect more plush.

With a curse, Mac punched the side of his truck bed, adding one more dent to the collection. "How did you figure this all out, Covie?"

She blew out a frustrated breath. "Are you going to keep asking questions or are we going to go disintegrate a warehouse full of plush?"

"I vote for disintegrate," Oliver said.

"Okay, you're right. I suppose you have a plan?" Mac said.

Covie smiled and winked. "Of course I do." She turned serious as she revealed it. "Oliver and I will climb up into the rafters of the warehouse and contaminate the serum-making process with my blood. Mac, you recon the building, take out any plush that try to leave, and be available to help us out if we get into trouble."

"That's just crazy enough to work," Mac said.

"Here." Covie handed two tubes of her blood to him. "Take these just in case."

He tucked them into an inside pocket of his long pelt-covered coat. "Let's do this."

The three of them nodded to each other, and Mac took off at a jog, skirting around yard equipment as he headed toward the building.

Covie donned her backpack, leaving the machete behind with a nervous glance. It was too unwieldy—she didn't want it to clang against something or get her hung up on something and alert the plush to her and Oliver's presence. The trusty knife Mac had given her when they'd parted ways last time was tucked safely into her boot. Plus, she had other weapon-like instruments hidden away in her backpack. She grabbed a gardening fork out of the back of Mac's truck to add to it.

"Can I take this?" Covie asked.

"A gardening fork?" Mac replied. "Sure! Whatever suits your fancy."

She smiled.

"Where are we headed, exactly?" Oliver asked. "Just in case we get separated."

"We need to find the pail that has your blood in it."

"Okay." He nodded. "I've been thinking about that, actually. I bet it's behind the portable walls near where the boxes of serum were. The boxes we hid behind. It's one of the places on the ground floor we didn't get to earlier, because we went in the opposite direction."

Covie clapped him on the back. "I bet you're right."

"One more question." Oliver looked over at the warehouse. "How are we going to get up in the rafters?"

CHAPTER FIFTY-TWO

Covie had already figured out how to get up to the rafters. And now that it was dark, she was sure it would be easier. "I noticed a ladder on the side of the building where the dump trucks line up. It goes to an opening at the top of the building, like a vent or something." She grinned. "Just the right size for two kids to crawl through."

"Excellent," Oliver said, bobbing his head like a '90s surfer dude.

I'm really starting to like this kid, Covie thought. "Let's go."

They waited until the lone dump truck dropping off its load drove away before sneaking over to the ladder—which neither of them could pull themselves up on, as the bottom rung hung about five feet off the ground. "Stay here," Covie said. She snuck around the corner to the rear of the building and brought back an empty crate.

It was the perfect height for them to stand on and reach the ladder. Once they were inside, Covie's stomach lurched. The metal rafters were wide, but not wide enough for as high up as they were. She didn't realize until that moment how scared of heights she was. A fall to the concrete floor below wasn't likely to kill them, but serious injury would result. The pounding of her heart in her ears made it hard for her to get her bearings. She squeezed her eyes shut and held on for dear life.

"Move it, Covie," Oliver whispered from behind her. "We just need to go right over there."

She forced her eyes open to look where he was pointing. It really wasn't far. They just needed to cross about ten of the rafters. Covie took a breath and wiped her forehead on her shoulder. *You can do this, Covie White*, she thought to herself.

About halfway over, just as her confidence was starting to build, her backpack shifted and she let out a short scream as she grabbed onto a vertical post to steady herself. She and Oliver looked down at the plush working below them. It didn't appear as if any of them had heard her above the noise of the machinery surrounding them. Covie leaned her head against the post she gripped with all her might, took a couple of slow breaths, then continued steadily on until they were directly above the room made up of mobile partitions.

"You were right, Oliver," she whispered with a weak smile. She stared down at the familiar steel pail containing his blood, wondering at the sophisticated biological response it caused that turned stuffed animals into evil living beings. Covie carefully extracted a vial of her blood from a zipped pocket of the backpack. There were only two plush working in the room, and she waited for one of them to move away from the work table before dropping a small amount of her blood into the pail. A gray bear plush wearing a hard hat reached across the table as another drop fell from the rim of the open vial, landing on the outstretched arm of the plush. The hard hat clanked to the floor as the bear disintegrated into a pile of colorful ash.

Covie looked at Oliver, mirroring his widening eyes as they tried to conceal themselves in the shadows. She clamped her jaw tight, breathing unsteadily through her nose.

"Albert!" A donkey plush rushed over to where the hard hat lay. "What in the squish happened? Hey, guys! Get over here! Something happened to Albert."

A few plush gathered around the ash, including one wearing a red vest. "What happened here, Eddie?" the vest-wearing plush asked with authority.

"I . . . I don't know. He just . . . one minute he was fine, then . . . *poof.*" The donkey gestured to the colorful pile topped by the yellow hat.

The plush that was apparently a supervisor shook its head. "We'll need to report this to Plush Zero." It nudged the pile with its toe, then lifted the hat to look under it. "Someone get this mess cleaned up before it contaminates the serum."

Covie kept waiting for one of them to look up and discover them crouching in the shadows, but none of them did. Fortunately, they didn't survey the area to try to find a possible cause for the sudden demise of their coworker. She and Oliver sat still as stone, her tightened muscles cramping, until the commotion beneath them settled down and all that was left in the little partitioned room was the plush tasked with sweeping up the ash.

Due to the sweltering heat in the rafters, beads of sweat popped up on Covie's forehead and armpits. "Let's get out of here," she whispered, worried a drop of sweat landing somewhere below would expose them. She glanced back the way they'd come and frowned. The small opening to the outside had been covered.

Oliver followed her gaze and then pointed to his right

and whispered, "There's a ladder over there." He crawled to the next crossbeam and headed in that direction.

With a shaky breath, Covie followed him. She stopped at the crossbeam to wipe her sweaty palms on her pants and Oliver waited for her to catch up before continuing. How on Earth did those high-rise construction workers *walk* on these beams, hundreds of feet in the air?

Halfway to the ladder, Covie looked down and her hand slipped. She let out an involuntary grunt as her chest and chin hit the beam. Her arms and legs reacted instinctively, hugging the beam like the lifeline it was.

"Covie!" Oliver's frantic whisper sounded like a shout to her ears.

She forced her tightly shut eyes open and scanned the floor. A tall giraffe plush stopped, said, "Huh?" and looked around in dazed slow motion. Before it could look up, a plush in a red vest yelled at it to get moving and something about meeting the boss's quota.

Oliver reached the ladder and, with a look back to make sure she was behind him, stepped onto the top rung.

CHAPTER FIFTY-THREE

Oliver was almost halfway down the ladder when Covie reached it. She stepped onto the top rung, pulling on the sides of the ladder to test its sturdiness. It rattled, and flecks of rust fell, a few of them landing on Oliver's head. He made it to the bottom and dropped the rest of the way to the floor.

As Covie reached the halfway mark, a loose bolt fell to the cement with an echoing *clank* and the rung bearing the weight of her right foot shifted. "Aaah." A small sound forced its way out of her before she could clamp her lips together.

The area they'd descended into was deserted and poorly lit, but noise traveled in the metal building.

"Go see what that was!" a husky voice commanded.

"Hurry, Covie," Oliver whisper-yelled.

She rushed down the last few rungs, then jumped to the ground beside him. He grabbed on to her hand and dragged her as shuffling feet hurried toward them. He crawled into a large box half full of serum vials, pulling her with him. Some of the glass vials crunched beneath their weight, but it barely registered with either of them as they crouched low, holding their breath.

The plush sent to investigate the noise shuffled closer. "Hmm," it said, then grunted. Something scraped against the cement floor. "It was just a loose screw that fell off the ladder, boss!"

"You're a loose screw, you numbskull! That's a bolt. Now get back to work," the husky voice said.

Covie and Oliver stayed hunkered down for another minute. Then she peered over the edge of the box. "All clear. Let's go find Plush Zero. I have a present for him." She checked her pocket for the remaining tubes of her blood, relieved to find them there and intact.

They snuck about, hiding behind equipment as they searched. After fifteen minutes with no luck and a couple of close calls, Covie stopped behind a vacated forklift and sighed. "This is getting us nowhere. We need a plan."

"Do you know where Mac is?" Oliver asked.

"I have no idea."

They hid in silence for a moment, thinking. "Screw this," she huffed. "I'm just going to grab one of the little buggers and force it to tell us where Plush Zero is."

Oliver shrugged. "That's as good an idea as any."

Covie watched the activities in the warehouse for several minutes before acting on her plan. She noticed a section where unused equipment was parked and stacked. The old green industrial hanging light above it flickered from dim to less dim, but never bright, and there seemed to be no activities going on there. One of the plush guards plodded near the area every few minutes as part of its rounds, but none of the others even came close. When the guard circled away from the deserted equipment, she tapped Oliver's arm and whispered, "Follow me."

Stopping to hide behind boxes and shelves along the way, Covie wished she and Oliver had plush disguises—as disgusting as it was to be inside one of their smelly pelts—so they could move about more freely. They reached their destination with only a minute to spare, as the guard came tromping over to make its rounds.

Covie darted from behind a large machine and grabbed the medium-sized bear around the chest with one arm, covering its toothless mouth with her other hand, and dragged it back to where Oliver waited in their hiding spot. He took the flashlight/taser from the guard's belt and Covie hung the plush on a sharp hook, eye level with her.

The plush bear squirmed, trying to disengage itself from the hook puncturing through its vest and into its upper back. "Who are you? Whaddya want?"

"Where is Plush Zero?" Covie asked.

If the bear's plastic eyes could have widened, she was sure they would have, but instead, its mouth hung open briefly before twisting into a sneer. "You're that girl that killed Window, ain't ya?"

"Tell me where I can find Plush Zero." She wasn't in the mood to have a conversation with this creature.

"I ain't tellin' you anything."

"Show him what we can do," Oliver said.

Covie pulled the Bowie knife out of her boot and lopped off the bear's paw.

It grimaced, but laughed. "Is that all ya got? I've had worse than that done to me." It wiggled its leg that, from the knee down, was a clawed plush dinosaur leg, sewn on with large, uneven stitches of red yarn.

"Watch closely," Covie said. She handed the gory paw to Oliver and dripped a tiny amount of her blood on it. As soon as the blood hit the plush fabric, the paw disintegrated into ash. "That's what'll happen to you if you don't talk."

The fuzzy brown fur turned a shade lighter and the

plush bear choked and spluttered. "H-help! S-someone help! Humans in—"

Covie held the tube of blood over its head. "Quit your yelling and tell me where Plush Zero is or, *poof*, pile of ash, and I move on to the next plush."

"No, no. Don't—don't *poof* me. That ain't necessary. The boss is usually in one of the observation rooms up on the second floor. If he ain't in one, then he's in the other one. Just take the stairs. There's catwalks that go from one to the other." The plush guard spoke so fast, Covie could hardly keep up. It pointed to a locked door behind them. "That'll get ya to the stairs."

"Thank you for your cooperation." She tipped the tube of blood until a drop dangled from the rim.

"No! I—" The plush's protest was cut short as the drop fell and it crumbled into colorful ash.

Covie snatched the key card from the guard's vest and turned toward the locked door.

"Uhh, Covie," Oliver said. "I think they know we're here."

CHAPTER FIFTY-FOUR

The clatter and hum of equipment ceased. Covie peered between two big metal machine parts and watched as the plush workers gathered in the center of the warehouse floor. The clown plush, still holding its clipboard, stood before them. "Someone or some*thing* is messing with our processes here, and we need to find them. Split up into your work groups and each group go with one of the guards to search. If you find the culprit, capture, don't kill. We'll need to do some interrogation."

Covie shuddered at the creepy clown smile. "Come on." She gestured for Oliver to follow her. Using the key card, she opened the door the now pile-of-ash plush had told them would lead to the stairs.

No wonder we couldn't find Plush Zero, Covie thought as they hurried through a maze of hallways trying to find the stairs. She'd had no idea about this part of the warehouse, full of offices and other rooms. She looked back to make sure Oliver was keeping up. He was right behind her . . . and a small group of plush was ten yards behind him. "Run," she said.

With a glance over his shoulder, Oliver obeyed.

"Stairs!" He pointed down a hallway to their left and they veered in that direction.

Covie used the key card to access the stairs and Oliver kicked a triangle doorstop under the door once it closed, hoping to slow down the plush on their tail. Covie booked it up the stairs, stopping on the landing to wait for Oliver. He had his hand pressed to his side and breathed heavily as he grimaced and grumbled, "I hate stairs."

Pounding echoed up the stairwell as the plush tried to force the door open. Covie and Oliver entered the room at the top, locking it behind them. "How did we not notice this room when we were up in the rafters?" she asked as she stared out the floor-to-ceiling windows looking out over the warehouse floor.

"Yeah." Oliver stood next to her, still breathing heavily. "We must have been too focused on not falling to our deaths or being seen."

"You're probably right. Plus, we were way over there." Covie pointed to the area where they'd crawled along the rafters. It would have been difficult for them to see this room. She turned about, surveying the messy desk and dusty shelves. "No Plush Zero in here."

"Nope. Because he's over there." Oliver pointed to a second observation room directly across the warehouse from them.

"Seriously?" Covie stared at the plush monkey sitting in a hot tub with a couple of females—at least one of them *human*. "Well, that's where we need to be." She eyed the metal grate of the catwalk connecting the two rooms and moved toward the door that opened up to it.

Rumbling footsteps pounded up the stairs, and a group of plush pushed the main door in, blocking Covie's and Oliver's access to both doors. She picked up a paperweight from the desk and hurled it through one of the windows, shattering it. She and Oliver climbed out onto a hydraulic platform lift, and she started pushing buttons, trying to get it started.

A plush minotaur jumped through the window, and Oliver batted it over the side of the lift. Another plush followed, and he was able to sling it to the ground as well. "Hurry up, Covie!"

"I'm trying!"

A group of three plush jumped Oliver at once. He batted one off the edge, but one jumped on his back and the other sank its teeth into his arm. "Ouch! Covie!"

The lift hummed to life, and Covie pushed the button to lower them to the ground. She pulled the knife from her boot and jabbed it in her arm with a wince before handing the blood-tipped weapon to Oliver. There was no time to mess with the blood tubes.

Oliver stabbed the biting plush, disintegrating it, then slashed over his head, into the eyeball of the plush on his back. He held his breath as the ash fell around him, not wanting to breathe any of it in.

Slowly, the lift lowered them through a cloud of colorful ash as an ever-increasing crowd of plush watched from the broken window they'd just escaped through. As the platform stopped on the ground, plush jumped from the observation room above, splatting to the cement around them, but jumping right up, uninjured. Covie shook her head as a few of them emitted a cute little playful "squeak" when they hit the floor.

She pulled her backpack around to the front and unzipped the main compartment to grab the gardening fork as they trotted across the warehouse floor. Plush came at them from all sides, and Oliver jabbed at them with the contaminated knife while Covie dipped the prongs of the gardening fork in the oozing blood of her arm. The plush were slow to learn, as a half-dozen of them were turned to ash before the rest backed off from the duo, covered in the colorful ashen remains of their coworkers.

With a clear path ahead, Covie and Oliver sprinted the rest of the way to the doorway marked "Stairs." She used the key card to open the door, and Oliver again wedged a doorstop beneath it before they charged up the stairs leading to the other observation room.

Covie hesitated at the top, just outside the door of the room where they now knew they'd find Plush Zero. She didn't have a plan. And she didn't have time to formulate one. She looked at Oliver, who shrugged as if reading her mind. "Let's do this," he said between heaving breaths.

The door clicked as she held the key card up to the electronic lock. They barged into the office, stopping a few steps inside, confused at the scene before them.

"What the what?" Covie murmured as she stared at the office full of junk. Cardboard boxes and sections of plywood spray painted to look like walls, shelves, curtains, and elaborate graffiti were arranged around the large room in a parody-like display of the big New York office of someone important.

A woman's giggle drew Covie's attention away from the cartoon-like decor, and she stepped around a faux wall, a gasp of surprise and disgust rushing from her throat at what she saw.

Plush Zero sat in a hot tub, surrounded by a couple of plush ladies and . . . Charlotte. A little plush seal crested the bubbling water and floated on its back while two small ducklings floated in circles around the seal.

CHAPTER FIFTY-FIVE

Plush Zero's back faced Covie, its bear-claw hand stroking the side of a red-lipped hippo plush's face as the hippo fluttered its outlandish sparkly eyelashes at the monkey. Charlotte's eyes jerked to Covie's just as Covie covered her mouth, too late to stifle the gasp that had already bounced off the cardboard walls.

Charlotte's surprised scream was followed by the shrieks of the two lady plushes, and the foamy water sloshed as the three of them scrambled to climb out of the hot tub. Covie flung her arm out to keep Oliver from exposing himself around the corner of the cardboard, but he dodged it, screeching to a halt at the sight of his dripping-wet mother stepping toward them wearing a neon-pink bikini—a size too small to appropriately contain her surgically enhanced bosom.

As water sloshed onto the tile floor, Plush Zero spun around, and his eyes narrowed at the two of them as recognition dawned on his face. "Don't let them get away!" he yelled, springing from the tub and snatching a gun off the desk.

The hippo plush circled around behind Covie and Oliver, with a tattered lamb plush and Charlotte blocking their way forward. "Covie? Oliver?" She glanced between them, mouth agape before twisting into a snarl. "What are you doing here? What are you doing with my kid?"

Covie's mama-bear protectiveness kicked in, and she grasped Oliver's hand—holding the gardening fork, tines pointed at Charlotte, in the other. Oliver's skin was cool and clammy to the touch, and his body trembled beside her.

Words forged by anger and betrayal tore from deep inside her, aimed at her former friend, spewing like lava in the small but terrifying voice of young Covie. "You evil, vile woman! How could you desert your son? Leave him to endure years of torture at the hands of these repulsive fluffy miscreants?!" She waved her arm around. "*Join forces* with the creatures that are destroying our world?!"

"Shut up!" Charlotte's face turned a deep shade of red. "Who in hades do you think you are to judge me?! You don't know what you're talking about!" She turned to Oliver and spoke in a falsely high voice. "Olly, honey, it's so good to see you."

With a furious tremor in his voice, Oliver responded, "Bull—"

"Enough!" Plush Zero interrupted, the barrel of the gun pointing first at Covie, then at Oliver. "Subdue them!"

Covie dived and rolled away from Charlotte and her lady-plush posse as they closed in. Somewhere behind the layers of graffitied cardboard walls, the door crashed against a real wall. The plush that had been chasing them across the warehouse piled through the open door. Covie pushed to her feet and raced toward Plush Zero, garden fork held in front of her like a knight's sword. Her foot skated out from under her when she hit a wet tile and a group of plush mobbed her as she hit the floor hard.

"Covie!" Oliver yelled.

Multicolored ash fell around her as she and Oliver disintegrated a few of the attackers. Covie gained her feet and met eyes with Plush Zero as he watched the fray from a short distance away. With a growl, she kicked off a penguin plush clinging to her leg and moved toward the monkey. Plush Zero's minions scrambled to surround him, protecting their boss from Covie's menacing gardening tool. Unable to get to him, she turned her attention to Charlotte, who stood off to the side, out of reach.

A large plush landed on Covie's back, wrapping its gangly arms around her neck. She reached back and grabbed it by the head, pulling it over and slamming it to the ground. Oliver gored it through the chest before Covie had time to pierce it with her meager weapon, but instead of disintegrating, it flopped around screaming and latched on to Oliver's hand, drawing it toward its mouth, where two teeth made of sharpened soda-can tops eagerly awaited.

Covie rammed the garden fork into the center of its face, the metal tines screeching against the tile through the resultant pile of ash.

"Why didn't mine work?" Oliver asked.

"It must not have any blood left on it." As more plush piled into the room, Covie turned to face them. "Hand me the knife." She once again plunged the tip into her arm, then handed it back to Oliver with its renewed plush-poofing power. She swiped the tips of her weapon through the blood and went to work on the plush closing in on them.

A tall figure emerged from the shadows of a cardboard wall. A small squeak issued from Covie's throat as the figure's profile came into view—a metal beak jutting out from a mask-covered face. "Mac," she breathed.

He met her gaze with his one visible eye, then put a long, thin tube to his lips beneath the beak of the plague mask.

What's he going to do? Covie thought. *Pied-piper the stuffed creatures with a tune on his flute?*

But when Mac puffed a short burst of air into the tube, the only sound was a muffled *thwack* as a small dart shot out, the sharp tip connecting with the side of a beloved cartoon-character plush's head, turning the character into a plume of ash.

"Dude!" Oliver yelled. "That's awesome!"

The cardboard walls shook and many of them crumpled as more and more plush pushed their way into the room.

"Where's the monkey?" Mac yelled between firing off the blow dart.

Covie looked to where she'd last seen Plush Zero, but a half-collapsed box was all she could see. "I don't know!"

With another puff of breath, Mac pulverized a jackrabbit plush, then said, "I'm going to guard the door. We can't let that thing escape!"

CHAPTER FIFTY-SIX

Walls collapsed around Covie and Oliver as an army of plush filled the room. Mac slammed the door and stood with his back pressed against it as he fought off a flock of geese plush with his sword. Covie lost track of him as a herd of farm-animal plush surrounded her, pushing Oliver farther away.

Wishing she had her machete, Covie jabbed at the crazed plush with the stupid gardening fork. Colorful ash filled her nose and eyes. Now she was just stabbing blindly around her. Out of the corner of her irritated eye, she saw a flash of bleached-blonde hair and a small patch of neon-pink material. She blinked some of the gritty plush remains away in time to see Charlotte disappearing into the maze of collapsed cardboard walls, dragging Oliver with her.

"No!" Covie's heart leaped in her chest. She hesitated only a moment before rushing to help Mac guard the door, afraid Charlotte would escape with Oliver.

With an echoing roar, Mac kicked the final goose with his steel-toed boot. It rocketed across the room, knocking down the last of the cardboard walls like a set of dominoes. Charlotte stood next to the large windows looking out over the warehouse, holding a struggling Oliver around the neck in a jiujitsu choke hold. He kicked back at her and scratched at her arm with his fingernails as his face turned red with exertion and rage. Charlotte's grip held strong, though, as she screeched at her son, "Stop fighting me, Oliver! I am your mother, and you *will* obey me, or else!"

Mac gripped Covie's arm to get her attention. She whirled on him, sure her eyes were wild and insane looking. "I have to—"

"You'll never get to him in time," he interrupted. "We need fire. Start the cardboard on fire, Covie."

"What? Why? I . . . I don't have any matches." She needed to get to Oliver.

"I thought you had everything in that backpack of yours." Mac shook his head. "Just . . . keep fighting while I think of something."

Plush Zero appeared next to Charlotte and Oliver by the window nearest the hot tub.

The hot tub!

Covie dove to the floor and army crawled over to it, leaving Mac to fend for himself. She ripped the side panel open, exposing the electrical wires and heater. Unsure if her desperate plan would even work or if it would kill her when she didn't know why Mac wanted a fire started in the first place, Covie pulled wires until one of them sparked in her hand. Plush piled onto her back, pulling at her clothes and hair. She flipped over, grabbed her weapon from where she'd dropped it next to her, and dispatched the attacking gang within seconds.

She pulled a piece of cardboard to her and touched the sparking wire to it. The old, crumbling paper ignited, and Covie pushed it away from her and rolled out of harm's way, leaving the sparking wire hanging out of the panel.

By the time she regained her feet, half the room was in flames.

A lumpy giraffe plush galloped past her, its tail aflame, and fell headfirst into the water of the hot tub. Plush screamed and ran about in a frenzy as the flames rose and smoke filled the room.

Covie backed up to where Mac stood by the door, watching the downed faux walls burn. "We need to get Oliver and get out of here," she said.

"Come on," he muttered under his breath, staring up at the ceiling.

"Mac!" Covie shook his arm. "What is wrong with you? We need to find Oliver and leave!"

He continued to stare at the ceiling.

Covie's voice increased in volume and hysteria. "What was the point of starting a fire to help us escape if we're just going to stand here?!"

Finally, Mac looked at her, his blue eye sparkling. He pointed to the ceiling. "That was the point."

Ice cold water hit Covie as the overhead sprinkler system kicked in. She bowed her head and rubbed water and soot from her eyes. When she glanced back up, plush all around her were disintegrating into wet piles of rainbow-colored ash. She turned her gaze to Plush Zero just as he puffed away into oblivion; the spiked ball replacing his tail rolled a few inches before stopping at Charlotte's feet.

"Mac . . . did you—"

"Did I put a couple tubes of your Phyzcoxin-infused blood into the fire suppression system for the warehouse? Why, yes, I did."

"Genius," she whispered as she watched the last of the plush in the room explode into multihued ash.

"You think you win by killing Plush Zero?" Charlotte screeched from across the room. A half-crazed laugh bubbled out of her. "Well, you're wrong, because I'm the real leader of this operation! That stupid monkey was just the second-in-command! This stunt of yours changes nothing!" Her eyes were wide, crazy rage etched on her pupils.

Covie stepped slowly toward her, trying to keep her voice calm. "You're wrong, Char. It's over. We have the ultimate weapon. Let go of Oliver."

A sneer tore across her face and she tightened her grip around his neck and whispered, "I'm going to kill Oliver and drain him of all his blood. I don't need him anymore. We cracked the code. We found the meteor. I have the same DNA sequence in me now."

CHAPTER
FIFTY-SEVEN

Who was this woman Covie thought she knew? How could she have been so fooled into thinking Charlotte was a good human being? Even though her blood was boiling with rage, she swallowed it down—Oliver needed her to be calm. She looked into his frightened eyes and stood taller amidst the falling water, faltering flames, floating ash, and smoke. If she kept Charlotte talking, maybe she and Mac could get close enough to help him.

"What do you mean *you* are the leader? How could you possibly have crafted"—Covie swept her arms in an all-encompassing arcing motion—"all of this?"

Charlotte's face relaxed from a sneer to a know-it-all smirk, and her grip on Oliver loosened a fraction. "I'm the one who booby-trapped that claw machine to get to Window—what happened to you was just an added bonus. *I* talked Window into kidnapping Tom and Chad and the other scientists." She barked out a short laugh. "And I talked *you* into getting Tom to destroy Tippy Toys by sharing their secret Safe Stuffing formula so Plush Zero and I could animate more plush!"

Stay calm. Covie's grip on the gardening fork tightened until it hurt. "Why, Char? I don't understand why you'd do this. What's in it for you?" While Charlotte looked briefly up at the ceiling, Covie took a step toward her.

"So we could take over the world, of course. I'll have the best of everything: houses, yachts, cars, jewels, everything."

Mac growled a curse under his breath and moved forward too, but Charlotte didn't notice. Now that she'd started talking, she seemed unable to stop herself from confessing her own genius. "It's such an easy way to create a loyal army of soldiers that just keep going and going, even with missing body parts!"

Covie's eyes slipped to Oliver's again. His tight jaw tremored just a little and angry tears mingling with water from the sprinklers made trails down the ash on his face. He stilled his struggling and took heaving breaths.

Returning her gaze to Char, Covie couldn't keep the disgust from her voice. "What about Oliver, Charlotte? How could you do this to your son?"

A flicker of a frown crossed her face, quickly replaced with the earlier smugness. "I don't know how you found him or found out who he is, Covie, but just so you know, I *was* a good mom, before all of this."

"Hmph," Mac grunted. "I bet."

She narrowed her eyes at him. "Who are you to judge me, Darth Vader wannabe?! Those military doctors are at fault here. They told us Olly had to stay at the hospital and convinced me and my husband that the only way to save him was to give him growth hormone inhibitors, so we agreed to it. That's why he's such a runt for his age."

Oliver grimaced.

"A good mom wouldn't have just deserted him and let Plush Zero and his crew use him however they wanted."

Covie fought to stay in control. She really wanted to rip Charlotte's eyes out with her gardening fork.

"I didn't *desert* him. I still visited him."

"But you let them hold him captive and put him in a coma!" Covie yelled. "You let them siphon his blood like vampires! He was just a means to an end for you!"

Charlotte swiped at the wet blonde hair falling into her face and shrugged. "I never wanted to have a kid in the first place. It was Chad's desire, not mine." She tightened her arm around his neck for an instant. "But since the kid ended up being of some use . . . who was I to stop it?"

"You're his *mother*! It was your job to protect him! And what about Chad? Where has he been during all this?" Covie's whole body shook.

"Oh, stop being so judgmental, Covie. Chad was asking too many questions, so I told him the kid died and they had to keep his body for *science*." An evil smile made her eyes sparkle. "Maybe I'll do a better job as a mom with your Emily."

Mac grabbed Covie's shoulder to keep her from lunging at the woman as she yelled, "Stay away from my daughter!"

"Daughter?" Mac questioned.

"Nah. I don't think I will." Charlotte ignored him. "Your unfortunate incident with the claw machine was an unintended bonus. With you in child form, I can finally have Tom. I've always loved him, you know, since the day we moved into the neighborhood."

"Child form? Covie, what—" Mac looked from her to the nearly-naked woman.

Covie shook her head, eyes glued to Charlotte's. "You . . . you can't have him. You're already married. He loves *me*." *Doesn't he?*

Charlotte snorted with laughter. "He loves Covie *the*

woman. Not you, little girl. I'll help him get over the wife who supposedly deserted him and his daughter. And as for Chad, I'll divorce him *and* take him for all he's worth. Such an idiot of a man."

"What are you two talking about?" Mac demanded.

"Not now, Mac!" Covie yelled.

The dripping-wet skin of his mother's bikini-clad body, coupled with her grip loosening as she talked, gave Oliver just enough leverage for his renewed struggles to catapult himself out of her grip. He lunged forward and grabbed the still-sparking wire connected to the hot tub, then twisted like a world-class gymnast and jabbed the live wire into Charlotte's bare side. She stiffened, her face frozen in a nasty snarl, and fell into the hot tub with a splash.

As soon as the wires were no longer in contact with her body, she regained her ability to move, thrashing around in the water. Her limbs shook and she gasped for air when she finally righted herself. She struggled to climb out of the tub with her weakened muscles. "You little brat!" she sputtered.

Oliver stepped toward her. "You never loved me. You left me to die. You let my blood get taken over and over. You *used* me like a lab rat."

She reached for him. "Please, I do love you."

"No you don't!" he said, lowering the sparking wires to the water's surface.

Charlotte waded forward. "It's not what you think, Olly. We can do this together. Now that I have the same blood as you, we can be together. I did it for you."

Whatever nonsense she was trying to sputter didn't faze Oliver. Covie stood at the ready. Charlotte put her foot on one of the hot tub seats and jumped toward him. At the last minute, Oliver dropped the sparking wires into the water. "Liar!"

CHAPTER FIFTY-EIGHT

Oliver jumped back as the water flashed with electricity, the glow reflecting off the tears on his face. They watched as Charlotte convulsed and died, acrid black smoke rising from her skin and hair as she sank into the agitated water. With a loud *pop,* the hot tub grew quiet, electricity no longer flowing through its wires.

"Wow," Mac said. "That was ..." He shook his head.

Oliver ran to Covie and wrapped his skinny arms around her. She held him tight as he regained his composure. Mac stepped closer and put an arm around both of them as they watched the last weak flame in the room burn itself out. The overhead sprinklers shut off with a *clank.*

"Sh-sh-she-she's dead," Oliver sobbed.

"You did nothing wrong," Covie said. "You saved us. It's because of you we're alive."

Mac knelt down next to them. "You're a hero. You ended the plushdemic."

Oliver sniffed. "I did?"

Covie nodded.

"Yes," Mac said. "You did."

Covie didn't know what else to say, so she hugged him tighter. "Come on, let's get out of here."

She glanced back at the charred corpse that was once her best friend. Her lower lip quivered, and teardrops squeezed out of her closed eyes.

When they reached the warehouse floor, Mac scanned the area through the green lens covering his right eye. "There are a couple of plush hiding in those garbage cans and a couple more in the cab of that dump truck."

"How does he know that?" Oliver whispered to Covie.

"His mask isn't just a fashion statement," she answered. "That lens reads plush signature and lets him see them through things and far away."

"Cool." The admiration in his voice made her smile.

Mac kicked over the garbage can, tumbling the plush onto the wet floor. Two of them disintegrated almost immediately upon touching the contaminated water, and Covie stabbed the third with her gardening fork where it cowered on the lid.

They stopped at the truck. Covie opened the door and Mac shot darts dipped in her blood at the plush huddled inside, *poofing* them into nonexistence.

On their way across the dirt yard, they dispatched the few plush that darted from their hiding places to attack them. Mac scanned the area. "There are a ton of plush hiding out in the machinery and dumpsters. We should—" He looked down at Oliver, slumped against his side. "We should get Oliver somewhere safe, then I'll come back and kill them."

Covie took her first good look at Oliver since leaving the smoky, ash-filled warehouse. In the harsh lights shining down on the yard, she examined him. Beneath the grime, his eyes were sunken and his lips were white. "You okay, Oliver?"

"Tired." He held the Bowie knife out to her. "This thing's getting heavy. Plus . . . my mom."

She took the knife from him and slid it into the sheath in her boot. She shouldn't have let him come, but she wasn't sure she could have stopped him. When they reached her car, she held the passenger door open for him as he crawled into the seat. Her phone buzzed in the cup holder where she'd left it, and she reached over him to grab it.

"Hello?" Covie answered while Mac removed his mask for the first time since she'd met him. He wiped it carefully with a towel he'd pulled out of his truck, his back to her.

"Covie? This is Dr. Mary. Sorry to call so late."

"No problem. I'm up."

"Good. I just wanted to let you know that I talked to my brother's friend, who's a five-star general. The Army is preparing two Apache helicopters equipped with missiles laced with a solution I created made with your blood and Phyzcoxin. They just need to know where to send them."

Covie gave the doctor the location of the warehouse and added, "We killed most of them inside, but there are still plenty hiding out in the yard."

"Thanks, Covie. They will be there within minutes, so if you're still nearby, I urge you to leave now."

"Will do, Doctor. Thank you." Covie ended the call and looked up at the back of Mac's head, a mess of wet, thick brown curls sticking out all over. "Hey, Mac, we need to skedaddle. The Army is coming to finish the job."

He'd removed his mask and turned to face her. His

ice-blue eyes held a modicum of disbelief. "Really? How'd you arrange that?"

"Uhh . . ." Words formed slowly as she took in his appearance, a little surprised that he was relatively good looking. She wasn't sure what she'd expected—maybe a grotesquely mutilated, scarred face he felt he needed to cover up with a bizarre mask. She shook her head, hoping to rattle her thoughts back into order. "Sorry . . . I've just never seen you without your mask."

His mouth twitched into a split-second smile, and he ran a hand through his messy hair. "Yeah. I guess you haven't."

"So anyway, my doctor is the one who got the Army involved. Let's head over to the abandoned military hospital. There are still medical supplies there we can use to treat our wounds."

Mac nodded. "I'll follow you."

The *thwack thwack thwack* of helicopter blades sounded in the distance as he followed her onto the deserted road in his truck. The lights of the two Apaches came into view and flew over them a few minutes later, headed toward the warehouse. The sky lit up behind them as multiple ear-splitting explosions cracked the air. Oliver twisted in his seat to watch the devastation Covie could only glimpse in her rearview mirror.

"Holy crap!" he exclaimed with more energy than she'd thought he could gather. "They flattened it! The whole warehouse is gone."

CHAPTER FIFTY-NINE

The dim lights in the hallway of the hospital flickered as Covie led Mac and Oliver through the maze of junk back to his old room. They picked up first-aid supplies on the way, and she pulled a flashlight out of her soaked backpack in case the electricity failed completely.

"This is where they were keeping Oliver?" Mac kicked a broken rolling chair to the side of the hallway.

"Yeah. Great, right?" Covie's voice dripped with sarcasm.

Upon reaching Oliver's old room, she handed him a hospital gown and some scrub bottoms. "Change out of those wet coveralls and get up on the bed so I can change your dressings and attend to any new wounds." She looked at Mac. "We'll wait in the hall."

Mac shut the door behind them and looked at Covie with narrowed eyes. "You know, I wondered why a young girl would have such a grown-up vocabulary and just chalked it up to you being smart and out on your own. But that's not it, is it, Covie? That conversation you and the kid's mom had . . ." He tilted his head to the side. "You ready to tell me the truth?"

"It's kind of a crazy story."

"Crazier than what we've already been through together?"

Covie grinned. "I guess not." She told Mac about the claw machine incident and waking up in the body of an eleven-year-old.

"Whoa. That is pretty insane. But it explains two things: why you speak like an adult, and your obsession with that specific claw machine." He ran a hand through his hair. "So how old are you, really?"

"Don't you know you aren't supposed to ask a woman her age?" she teased. "Let's just say I'm in my thirties, and I'd *really* like to be again."

"Yeah," Mac said quietly, "I bet."

"I'm ready!" Oliver called from the room.

"Does the kid know?" he asked.

Covie nodded and opened the door.

She took off the old dressing on Oliver's abdomen and arm and cleaned the wounds as best she could before applying new bandages. "You need the one on your bottom changed too. Do you want me to do it?"

"No way! I'll do it myself."

Covie handed him the cleaning wipes and a new bulky dressing and sent him in the room's disgusting bathroom with instructions.

"That kid's been through some things," Mac said sadly as he stared at the closed bathroom door.

"You could say that."

Covie emptied her backpack onto the bedside table. Most of their remaining food was ruined, soaking wet and mushy. All that was salvageable was one can of fruit cocktail and a couple of small cans of Vienna sausages. "Dinner and dessert." She looked from the sausages to the dented fruit can and sighed.

"Here," Mac said, dropping a bag he had draped

over his shoulder onto the bed, "let me add a few courses to your gourmet meal." He dumped out multiple packages of snack food, ranging from cookies and fruit snacks to crackers and cheese. And bottles of water.

"Ahh, bless you!" Covie reached for a bottle of water and twisted the top off before gulping half of it down.

The three of them sat around the bed and ate. Oliver was quiet while Covie and Mac talked. "You okay, Oliver?" she asked him.

He shrugged and looked down at his hands. "So you know my dad?"

"I do."

"Do you think he's like . . . *her*? I mean, I remember him coming to the hospital before the plush took over. He came a lot. He played games with me and stuff."

Covie put her hand over his. "Your dad is a good man, from what I know. It sounds like your mom lied to him about you . . . about a lot of things. He's going to be so happy to find out you're alive."

"Do you think so?"

"I do think so."

His voice turned to barely a whisper. "Even though I . . . k-killed my mom?"

"I think he'll understand, Oliver." Covie put her arm around his shoulders.

Mac chomped on the cracker in his mouth, then swallowed and said, "The Army *did* just blow that building up with her inside it. You could just tell him they killed her."

"Mac—" Covie started.

Oliver shook his head. "I couldn't do that. Even if he believed me, *I* would know the truth. I have to tell him."

"I agree. That's too big of a burden for you to bear

alone, and trying to keep it a secret from your dad would make it worse." She pulled him closer to her side.

Looking so much younger than his fifteen years, Oliver gazed up at her with moisture in his tired eyes. "If he doesn't want me, can I come live with you?"

"Absolutely . . ." Covie frowned. "If I can ever get my real body back and return to my family."

"You will." He yawned. "I'm sure of it."

"It's late," she said. "Oliver, you take the bed, and I'll sleep on the floor." She looked at Mac, unsure of his plans.

"I have something I need to do. I'll be back in a while." Mac shouldered his now-empty bag and headed to the door, plush pelts swaying as he walked.

Covie watched him leave, then turned to Oliver. "Let's get this bed cleaned up so you aren't sleeping on cracker crumbs."

"Uhh, Covie?" He crossed his arms over his chest. "I'd rather sleep on the floor with you. This bed has bad vibes."

Sadness at all he'd been through caused a lump to form in her throat, but she smiled and nodded. "Okay." She spread a couple of thin hospital blankets on the floor and they lay down, covering up with the bed curtain she tore down again.

Covie and Oliver fell asleep next to each other, using the dead, gutted bear-plush nurse as a pillow.

CHAPTER SIXTY

A giant plush bear, with human arms bulging with muscles the size of a VW Bug, stomped toward Covie, smashing everything in sight. Bones crunched as its enormous iron foot came down onto the hot tub where Plush Zero, Window, Sharkey, and Charlotte sat drinking champagne. The bear-man picked up three claw machines stacked atop each other and slammed them against a squealing carousel with mutated plush instead of horses. It reached for a plush octopus as it tried to slither beneath a fun-house car, plucking it up by a tentacle before crushing it in its man-fist, inky liquid mixed with bloody stuffing oozing between its fingers. The Kong-sized bear-man plush spun a dilapidated Ferris wheel, then turned to Covie with a maniacal grin, pointing at her as the Ferris wheel wobbled and squeaked.

Covie jerked awake and groaned, her sore muscles protesting the movement. As she rubbed her eyes, she realized the squeaking from the nightmare hadn't stopped when she woke up. Oliver stirred beside her. She whirled to face the sound, expecting to see a half-human plush bearing down on her. Tears sprang to her eyes and her hand fluttered to her chest as Mac wrestled a hand truck with a claw machine strapped to it through the hospital room door—one with a purple narwhal and a purple unicorn sticker affixed to the glass. THE claw machine!

Forgetting about her stiff muscles, Covie jumped to her feet and ran to help him get the unwieldy dolly over the threshold. Oliver joined in the effort, and he and Mac positioned it near an outlet where the inactive monitors were plugged in, while Covie clapped her hands and jumped up and down. Mac pulled the dolly out from under the load and rolled it out of the way while Oliver unplugged one of the monitors and plugged in the claw machine.

Colored lights inside the glass and running along the top of the outside of the machine blinked to life and the claw twitched into motion, swinging back and forth as it moved to reset itself in the center of the glass enclosure. Soft chimes played a tune, and Covie reached for the unicorn and narwhal stickers, confirming with a touch that this was the right machine. Still pressing her fingers against it, she turned to Mac. "But it's empty. There aren't any plush in it."

Mac pulled a small Safe Stuffing walrus plush from his duster with a combination grin and grimace on his face, and placed it inside the machine through a hatch in the back. "I fixed it so you don't need money or a card to work it." He gestured to the joystick and stepped back, allowing Covie to play the most important game of her life.

What if it didn't work? What if she'd been wrong about everything? About what had caused her transformation and how to reverse it. What if this machine was no longer booby-trapped? Her hand trembled as it hovered just inches away from the joystick, unable to move forward as her mind tumbled endlessly.

"Come on, Covie, just do it already!" Oliver said.

With a nervous laugh, she gripped the controller and maneuvered the claw above the plush walrus. She held her breath as she pushed the button to release the claw. It landed on the back half of the plush, and Covie's heart skipped as the claw closed on the walrus's tail and started to rise. Before it had risen halfway, the plush slipped from its loose grip and tumbled back to the bottom. "Dang. Missed."

"Try again!" Oliver said.

Covie pushed her held breath out through pursed lips and then inhaled deeply. Gripping the controller, she tried again. And again, the walrus slipped through the claw.

"I always hated these things," Mac said, leaning against the wall. "They're rigged to make sure you don't win too often."

"Yeah," Oliver agreed. "Me and my friends spent all of our pooled allowance trying to win a signed football once."

"Did you end up getting it?" Covie guided the claw toward the plush for a third attempt. "Crap!" she cursed as it missed completely this time.

"They need to make these things with Wolverine claws," Mac said. "Then you could just drop it down and let it stab whatever prize you want."

Oliver laughed. "Or maybe we should call Santa Claws to come help. Get it? Santa *Claws*?"

"That's just *claw*ful, Oliver." Covie took a break, shaking her hand.

"Whatever," Oliver scoffed, "it was *claw*some."

She rolled her eyes and Mac chuckled.

"And," Oliver said, "to answer your question, we *did*

end up getting the football—and I just remembered the trick!"

"What trick?" Covie asked.

"They do something with the glass to make it look like the claw is in the right position when it really isn't. But if I stand over here"—he moved to one side of the machine—"and look through the glass, I can see the real position and guide you to it."

"Okay." Covie nodded. "Let's try it."

She steered the claw with the joystick, moving it to where she thought it was dead center over the walrus plush.

"Move it toward the back a little more," Oliver instructed. "Good! Now to the left just a little. Stop! That's the spot. Drop it."

Biting her lip, Covie pushed the drop button.

CHAPTER SIXTY-ONE

The claw dropped dead-center over the walrus plush and closed. Covie held her breath while it grabbed and lifted the walrus. Looking at her new friends, tears formed in her eyes as the claw slid across the track to deliver the plush to the hopper.

The three remained silent while Covie put her hand into the prize drawer and retrieved the walrus. She clutched it to her chest and closed her teary eyes, her heart fluttering like it had transformed into a butterfly.

A moment passed in silence, then Oliver gasped. Covie opened her eyes . . . and looked *down* at him. She stood at five-foot-ten again. And the room grew suddenly drafty. She looked down and cursed—she'd split through the little girl clothes and stood before Mac and Oliver in nothing but a few tattered rags that had managed to hang on. Heat rushed to her face as she covered her chest with an arm and her lower parts with the walrus plush.

"Shoulda thought of that ahead of time," she said. She was just glad she hadn't been wearing the kid-sized boots—they wouldn't have given way so easily.

Mac picked up the curtain she and Oliver had used

as a blanket while they slept and wrapped it around her, his eyes never straying from hers as he did so, thankfully.

Oliver mumbled, "Be right back," and hurried out of the room, returning a minute later with a pair of old, ratty scrubs for her.

The boys turned their backs while Covie put the scrubs on.

"Okay, you can turn around now." A lingering warmth to her cheeks let her know that the embarrassed blush remained. "Thanks, you guys, for helping me cover up."

"I didn't see anything," Oliver rushed to say, but the flush of his own skin said otherwise. He shrugged. "Not much anyway. I looked away real fast."

"As did I," Mac said. "And you're welcome. My mama raised me to be a gentleman."

"Did she raise you to be a mask-wearing weirdo too?" Oliver teased as he grinned up at the two adults.

"Ha!" Mac laughed. "No, that's all me."

"Well," Covie said, "weird or not, young or not, it doesn't matter to me. You guys are two of the toughest people I've ever met, and I'm happy to call you both my friends."

"Ditto." Mac nodded.

"What does that mean?" Oliver asked.

"Back at ya. Same here. Me too. Likewise. I agree with what you said, but in reference to you, not me." Mac ticked synonyms off like a thesaurus.

"Oh, well, ditto for me too," Oliver said. "But can we still be friends now that you're all grown up, Covie?"

"Of course we can." Her voice quivered on the last word, and she pulled Oliver to her in a tight mom hug.

With a huff, Mac joined them, wrapping them both in his plush pelt-covered arms as he grumbled, "Haven't hugged a single soul in years and you two have me doing it twice in less than twenty-four hours."

Oliver and Covie laughed. "Is it really that bad, tough guy?" she asked.

"I guess not. But don't you dare tell anyone. I don't want my enemies thinking I've gone soft."

"My lips are sealed," Covie said.

"Ditto," Oliver agreed.

They laughed and broke apart, and stood looking at each other.

"What now?" Oliver asked.

Covie tried to comb her fingers through her ratty hair, but they got stuck in the tangles. "I'm ready to go home and see Tom and Emily—and take a shower!"

"Oh man," Oliver said. "A shower sounds awesome."

"Yeah." Mac wrinkled his nose. "I didn't want to say anything, but you two smell awful." He waved a hand in front of his face for emphasis, then winked at Oliver.

"Rude!" Covie laughed. The group grew solemn in the silence that followed. "Well," she finally said, "I guess it's time for goodbye. I need to get back to my family. I'll take you to your dad, Oliver. He just lives down the street from me."

He nodded, eyes wide and scared.

"Where are you headed, Mac?" she asked.

"Back to the streets. Still lots of plush to rid the world of." His voice softened a little as he added, "I have your number, Covie. I'll be in touch. I promise."

She stood almost as tall as him now and knocked him back a step as she launched herself into him for another hug, her tears smearing against his coat. "You'd better. You've been so amazing. Thank you again."

"Don't get all mushy." His gruff voice hitched just a little, betraying his emotions. "And you're welcome. You were one tough little girl. I'm curious—and a little frightened—to see what you can do as a grown-up."

She snorted out a laugh and pushed away from him. He ruffled Oliver's messy hair. "Good luck, kid."

Oliver hugged him around the waist and Mac rolled his eyes. "Again?"

The spasm of his lips as he tried not to smile gave him away, though. He was liking all this affection, Covie could tell.

CHAPTER SIXTY-TWO

Chad Connelly stood in the doorway, a look of utter disbelief on his face. Covie had suggested that Oliver wait in the car while she broke the news of his return from the dead to his dad, and she was glad she had. Chad looked like he might pass out—his tan skin had turned ashen, and he opened and closed his mouth several times as if he'd forgotten how to form words.

Covie touched his arm. "Are you okay, Chad? Maybe you should sit down."

He wiped a hand down his face and swallowed, finally finding his voice. "How? He's alive! Where has he been? Does Char know?"

"That's all his story to tell. I just thought you might need a warning before he just knocked on your door."

"Where is he?" His eyes shot to her car parked in front of his house. "Is he here?"

Covie nodded and waved for Oliver to get out of the car.

Before his foot even touched the ground, his dad bounded off the porch. "Olly!" Chad met him on the lawn and swept him into an embrace, sobbing into Oliver's dirty hair. "I missed you so much. This is a miracle. Oh, Olly, I love you so much."

Oliver buried his face in his dad's neck and cried.

"You're so young," Chad said.

"It's a long story," Covie said. "I'll fill you in soon. But I've got to go see Tom and Emily."

She wiped her own face of tears, patted Oliver on the shoulder, and whispered, "Told you," before she went back to her car.

She got in the driver's side and watched them for a few more moments before pulling down the street and into her own driveway. It felt like it had been years since she'd been here, even though it had only been . . . she had no idea how long she'd been gone. A week? Longer? Shorter?

Covie took a deep breath and exited her car. She stopped at the door, fresh tears springing to her eyes as she gazed at Tom through his office window, oblivious to her presence as he worked at his computer. She smiled at the familiar way he tapped his pen on the desk as his eyes squinted in concentration.

Heart pounding, Covie opened the door. Emily, sitting on the floor doing homework, looked up, her face lit with a huge smile. "Mom!" She pushed up off the floor, ran to Covie, and jumped into her open arms, wrapping all four limbs around her. "I missed you!"

"Oh, Em! I missed you too. I love you so much."

"I love you too, Mommy." Emily pulled back and wrinkled her nose. "But you kinda stink."

Covie laughed and hugged her tighter as Tom joined them, embracing them both in his strong arms.

EPILOGUE

From atop the hill, Covie, Mac, and Oliver lay hidden in the tall grass as they watched a group of plush talking in the meadow below. Tom sat in Mac's truck, pressing a night-vision spotting scope to his left eye. He held a walkie-talkie close to his lips.

"Looks like there's a group of ten or so down there," Tom said, holding the walkie-talkie button down.

"Okay," Covie said, "sounds good."

She loved spending time with Tom doing their newfound hobby: slaying pockets of plush. On nights and weekends, of course.

The plush had gone into hiding ever since the discovery of the plush-killing agent made from Covie's Phyzcoxin-infused blood. SynthNA, the company producing it in massive quantities, even named it after her with a suggestion from Tom: CoveSynth.

The government had launched a large-scale operation to rid the world of the animated plush, but were only concentrating on sizable groups of the fiends. So Covie, Mac, Tom, and Oliver had taken it upon themselves to root out the smaller clusters and individual plush. And they were good at it. Covie glanced with a grim smile at the newest pelt Mac had added to his duster—an octopus that used to be a puppet. He'd gotten to the mad scientist at last, choosing to kill it the old-fashioned way so he could keep his pelt trophy.

"Attack on three," Mac whispered. "One. Two. Three."

The three friends rushed the group—Mac with his kitchen knife, Covie with her machete, and Oliver with the Bowie knife, all infused with CoveSynth. The plush fought back with their meager weapons, but rusty forks and tree limbs were no match for the trio. Before they'd even broken a sweat, all that was left of the plush were multiple piles of colorful ash.

Oliver slid his knife back into its sheath at his side. "We should really come up with a name for ourselves."

Covie handed out bottles of water. "Do you have any suggestions?"

"Stuffy Slayers?" Oliver suggested.

"Plush Pulverizing Posse—PPP for short." Mac took a long swig of his water.

Covie wrinkled her forehead. "Not bad. But how about Cove's Crew?"

"Oh! I've got a good one!" Oliver's face glowed with health now that he was back with his dad and being well taken care of.

Covie had been so relieved when Chad decided to stay in the house down the street from her and Tom. He'd started dating Penny, one of the lab techs working on the cure in Biotoy. Tom and Chad kept their jobs at Tippy Toys' Biotoy division and concentrated on a new line of slime-polymer action figures. Cove had grown rather close to Oliver and couldn't stand the thought of him moving away. Plus, he adored playing big brother to Emily.

"Let's hear it," she said.

Oliver held his hands out in dramatic fashion. "Association of Stuffy Hunters—ASH. Get it? Because we turn them to ash!"

The group sauntered back to the truck as Mac removed his helmet.

"Hey, Tom," Covie said. "Any more leads for tonight?"

"I got one more," he said. "There's a hoard of the little buggers that took up residence in that Stop a Sec you used to go to."

"How fitting," Covie said.

"But first," Tom said, "I want to publically apologize again about how I treated you when you were, you know, younger."

"You've already apologized to me—that night."

"I know, but I want to apologize to you and our friends. I know I didn't support you—or you guys, for that matter," he said, looking at Oliver and Mac. "I'm sorry. I need to be more open and understanding that things sometimes aren't what they seem, especially in this day and age."

"No worries," Mac said. "All's good in this hood."
Oliver chuckled.
Covie stepped in and hugged her husband. "I love you, Tom."

As a kid, Tyler H. Jolley always had a knack for storytelling. When he grew bored of old fables, he created his own exciting and unique worlds. Many years later, he still had so many new ideas and stories swirling in his head, but with nowhere to share it. That's when he put his pencil to paper and let the creative juices flow.

His debut novel, *Extracted*, came out in 2013 and swiftly became an Amazon Best Seller and Spencer Hill Press Best Seller. *Prodigal and Riven*, the second and third books in The Lost Imperials series were released in May of 2015.

After a brief hiatus he restructured and returned to writing. His Adventurous Ali series has received much praise. To date, he's released four in the series.

When he's not writing, you can find him at his orthodontic practice, mountain biking, or on the hunt for the perfect doughnut.